Virtue Inverted

Piers Anthony

&

Kenneth Kelly

Virtue Inverted
Copyright © 2017 by Piers Anthony & Kenneth Kelly

Cover Art & Design:
Mitchell Bentley, Atomic Fly Studios
Interior Formatting:
Niki Browning
Editor-in-Chief:
Kristi King-Morgan
Editors:
Kristi King-Morgan
Ally Fell

Printed in the United States of America

First Printing, 2017

ISBN-13: 978-1-947381-00-1
ISBN-10: 1-947381-00-8

Dreaming Big Publications

www.dreamingbigpublications.com

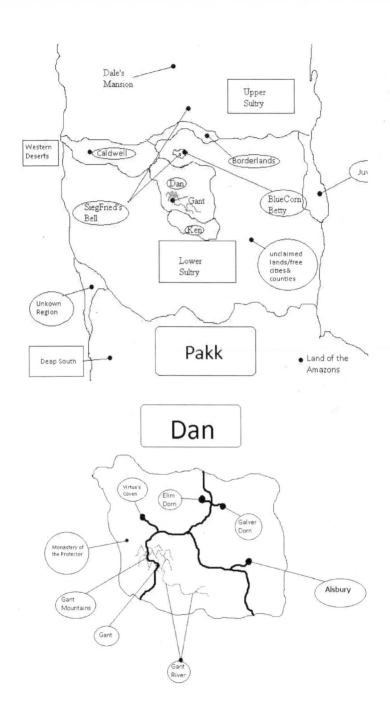

Dale's Mansion

Upper Sultry

Western Deserts

Caldwell

Borderlands

Ju\

Dan

Gant

SiegFried's Bell

BlueCorn Betty

Ken

Lower Sultry

unclaimed lands/free cities & counties

Unkown Region

Deap South

Pakk

Land of the Amazons

Dan

Virtue's Coven

Elim Dorn

Galver Dorn

Monastery of the Protector

Alsbury

Gant Mountains

Gant

Gant River

DEDICATION

To Kurt Van Wilt,
October 1,1949 to May 20, 2016.
May the muses be with you.

PREFACE

Few people who travel the main road through Gold Mulch Wood notice the little trail leading into the thick fir and conifer trees, and if travelers actually did take this passage into the forest, they would be even less likely to spot the fairy tale cottage that seemed to sprout out of nature itself. It was old by anyone's standards, with decades of vegetation camouflaging its structure. Sheet moss, Red Heather, Bluebells, and Violets coated the entirety of the roof and walls in thick layers, leaving only the door and windows uncovered. In the surrounding garden, there thrived other flora whose names even the proprietor had long forgotten: Fireweeds, Bleeding Heart, Pink Pussytoes, and Monkshood. And sitting on the side of the cottage, under a particularly large red caladium, was a little tow-headed boy in a red felt cap, playing with one of the giant mice that shared the garden with the humans. The old man watched him silently from the kitchen window, just a few feet from the child, and enjoyed the innocence of the moment.

The few people who knew about the secluded homestead – mostly fairies, gnomes, and other likewise isolated creatures – called him the Pawben, but his names were as vast and numerous as those of the stars in the midnight sky. He was an elderly man with a long white beard and crooked back, but if his years were known one might think he looked quite good for his age. Apart from his ugly gash of a mouth.

"Where's me pipe?" the man asked himself.

Turning from the window and setting down the half-eaten roll on the wooden counter, he walked to the snug sitting area by the fireplace, beside the ladder to the second floor bedroom where he slept. He sat down in a high-backed chair, almost as swathed in plants as the cottage, and found what he was searching for resting on the small table beside him. It was an ancient pipe, the stem splitting into two different bowls. In one he stuffed a homegrown blueberry tobacco; in the other, White Sage. The two together created a pleasant aroma as he leaned his head back, closed his eyes, and remembered…

CHAPTER 1

It was a scorching cold night in the mountain town of Gant. Most were asleep in their hovels, wrapped in blankets and animal furs, dreaming of a golden spring. Benny Clout, however, was wide awake. His older brother and guardian, Aiken, had been kicked out of the local Inn and Tavern, the Fox Den, and came home in a rage. He commenced with the usual, dragging Benny out of his bed, knocking furniture around, and shouting incoherent demands. Thus, the boy did what he always did: he kicked Aiken in the groin and hauled tail.

"You bloody pig!"

His brother's voice trailed off as Benny ran out the front door of their home and down the cobblestone streets. Benny wasn't wearing his coat, only a pair of cloth boots, tan leggings, and a loose fitting nightshirt. But Benny was hot blooded by nature, and the bite of frost felt great against his face as he ran downhill, passing through the market, past the chapel and apothecary, to the dark alley which led to the bar his brother had just come from. Aiken might have been prohibited for the rest of the night, but Benny wasn't.

The Fox Den was built with the same half-timbered

architecture as the rest of Gant, and was in fact two separate buildings, one on each side of the Gant River – for which the town was named – and attached to each other by a small hallway connecting the third floors. Benny had always been scared to walk across it as a younger boy, fearing he would fall through the floor to the water below, but now that he was a teenager he knew better.

"Ho, there!" A voice called.

Benny stopped just before the stone steps to the front door. He looked for where the voice came from, and saw his old friend Laughing Jack Baldwin, the innkeeper. He was standing on the small stone balcony that looked out on the river, and quickly came down the ramp to where Benny was. Ever since Benny's father died, Jack had been like a second father to him.

"Aiken's home safely, I presume?" he asked.

"Yep, and starting in on me like always."

"He didn't hurt you, did he?" Jack crossed his arms.

"He tried, but I set him down a notch."

"He'll tear your hide in the morning." Jack frowned.

"I doubt he'll remember!"

Jack laughed and put his arm across Benny's shoulder as they walked to the front door. As they entered the dining hall, Benny was greeted by the familiar smells of tobacco smoke and hops as the roar of laughter and drunken chatter filled his ears. He looked around at the familiar faces of town drunkards, a pair of mountain dwarves, and of course the Halfling bard, Nap, wearing his typical garb of polychromatic clothing. After one too many strokes on his lyre, a pugnacious she-elf threw her entire pint of ale into his little red face. With his hair plastered to his head and instrument hanging beside him, he waddled towards the kitchen.

"He always has a way with the ladies," Benny remarked.

As they walked back to the kitchen Benny gave one last look around his favored hang-out spot, and through the smoky haze saw the various murals painted on the walls depicting colorful scenes from local myths. His favorite was the legend of the rainbow gnomes, which depicted six little gnomes, each one's skin a different color of the color spectrum. They wore little red hats and were depicted as frolicking in a forest. However, when the smiling Benny laid his eyes on the two particularly sullen men sitting underneath the fresco, he quickly averted his gaze. He then entered the kitchen to hear the mouthful of complaints from the spirits-sodden halfling.

"You need to do something about that imp! I'm telling you, I don't get paid enough for this!" he squeaked.

"You don't get paid at all," Jack retorted, "and I've told you before not to hassle my customers."

"Oh…well…you should be paying me. I'm a world-class entertainer, I tell you! These sots just don't know good music when they hear it." Nap shook his sea-foam green coat, sending drops of stale beer flying into Benny's face.

"Remind me why I tolerate him?" Jack asked Benny.

'Cause you're an idiot."

Jack nodded in agreement and walked past the flustered Nap. He began ladling stew into wooden bowls from the large pot hanging in the fireplace and turned to Benny.

"Take this to the two gents sitting in the gnome seat, how about it?" Jack asked. Benny remembered the two creepy men and began to protest.

"You mean those two rogues in the corner?" Benny asked, swallowing hard.

4

"Yeah. They haven't touched a drop of ale, but they've nearly emptied my larder."

"They don't look overly friendly, Jack. I don't know…"

"They won't bite, trust me. They're old acquaintances of mine. They already paid for everything else. Tell 'em the soup's on me."

With that, Benny took the bowls and left as Jack went to the scullery. Benny was naturally shy, but over time he had grown to know most of the regulars at the inn. He could handle the usual rabble-rousers, even the likes of his brother, but he became quickly nervous around people he didn't know, especially two vagabonds like these. Their macabre appearance only worsened as he got closer. The one on the left was large and muscular, wearing a moldering leather jerkin over a tattered shirt. His ears were knotted like oak burls, and his short white-blond hair shot out in every direction. From the top of his crown clear down to his chin he had a hideous scar that seemed to split his face in half. His nose was missing, leaving two gaping holes in the center of his face. The scar had obviously split apart before healing completely, leaving a small hole just above his upper lip. As he chewed, food oozed out of it like pus from a cyst. As revolting as this man's face was, however, it was his companion who scared Benny the most. This man was dressed in robes of deep burgundy and velvet. He had long jet-black hair and a beard that was braided into thick cords, like a mop, from which hung coins, animal bones and other strange trinkets. A red floppy hat was pulled low over one side of his face, and what little bit of his face that wasn't covered with hair looked almost gray in color. Tobacco smoke rolled out of his mouth as he sucked on a twin-bowled pipe. As Benny stood there, holding the soup, the man grew annoyed and spit a mouthful of food back on his plate.

"Do we look funny to you, kid?" the scarred man asked.

"No, I was just…" Benny held out the soup.

"Then go ogle someone else!" he bellowed.

The man's voice was so loud it seemed to shake the very foundations of the building. Turning, Benny saw all the patrons had stopped to look in their direction. After a few seconds, they all began chuckling and returned to their prior engagements.

The man began to laugh, spitting food in Benny's direction. "Lighten up, boy!"

The other man chuckled silently, still puffing on his pipe.

"I…I was just bringing you the soup…compliments of Laughing Jack." Benny stammered.

"Ah, and how is the ol' spineless weasel?"

"Good, I guess."

"Youguess?" He lifted a glass of what looked like plain milk to his lips, "What's your name, boy?"

"Benny."

"You don't have a last name?" His face grew annoyed again.

"Clout…Benny Clout."

"Well, I'm Beranger." He placed a massive hand on his chest and then pointed to the silent man next to him, "and this is Cycleze."

The silent man nodded.

"A pleasure…" Benny nodded in return.

A tiny hand slapped Benny on the arm, and he almost jumped out of his skin. Benny relaxed when he saw it was only Nap, ready to serenade another customer.

"Hello, me lads! I'm Nap of Ken, famed bard, poet, and lyricist extraordinaire! You boys look like you could use a tune, so allow me..." he quickly began to strum an unpleasant melody.

A huge hand shot out and grabbed Nap by the neck.

"The next time you interrupt me, I'll rip your guts out and choke you with 'em!" He pushed Nap away so hard that the halfling fell to the floor, whimpering.

Beranger jumped to his feet, knocking the table forward several inches. Cycleze had a look of annoyance as his stew sloshed out of its bowl and into his lap. For a split second, Benny thought the man's eyes had flashed an eerie shade of turquoise and that a deep growl began to issue from his lips. But his attention was quickly diverted when he noticed Beranger advancing on the poor halfling. Several surrounding patrons began to cheer him on until Jack burst upon the scene, stepping in front of Nap and embracing Beranger.

"My old friend, it's good to see you! Hey Benny, go help Nadia clean the dishes, there's a whole heap of 'em. Now, you rascal..." With that the old friends began a roaring conversation of obscene gestures, vulgar stories, and hysterical laughter. Glad to be out of the conversation, Benny walked towards the kitchen.

Actually he was more than willing to work beside Nadia. Her blond hair was tied back in a ponytail and her body was completely covered by her barmaid uniform, but that did not conceal her nice figure and pretty face. He would have liked to have something more to do with her, but she had made it plain that at age eighteen she had better things in mind than a stripling boy two years her junior. So, he focused on his work, satisfied to be this close to her. Maybe some day--

"Stop it!" she snapped.

Benny paused with the pot he was scrubbing. "What?"

"You're thinking of me as if I'm your girlfriend. I'm not and never will be."

He wanted to protest, but couldn't, because she had him dead to rights. How did she know? "Sorry."

Partially mollified, she returned to the dishes. "It might be different if you were a real man."

Was this an opening? "Like who?"

"Like Dale."

Benny had no idea who Dale was and didn't want to advertise his ignorance, but he made a mental note to be alert for Dale. He almost thought he had heard the name before, but couldn't place it.

CHAPTER 2

It was almost morning by the time Benny left the Fox Den, Jack and his old comrades still living it up in the corner booth. He'd tried to wave goodbye to Jack, but he was far too preoccupied with Beranger and his silent companion. Nap was nowhere to be found, and the few patrons who hadn't gone home or checked into a room across the river were passed out drunk in the dining hall. Benny was surprised Jack didn't call for Liverwart, the mountain giant, to drag their unconscious bodies out of the building, but he was tired and didn't really care. The sun had begun to rise, but with the surrounding forests and mountains on either side, Gant remained in an almost eternal twilight.

Upon entering the small hovel he called home, Benny saw Aiken passed out on the floor by his bed. Benny tried to wake him, but he was incoherent and still hung over from his nightly binge drinking. Of all things, it was Aiken's job to travel to and deliver barrels of beer, mead, and food supplies from the neighboring town of Down Mountain to the Fox Den. Benny knew the hell he'd go through if Aiken stayed sober for more than a day, so after drawing water from the well outside he threw the contents onto Aiken. He jumped up like a bat out of hell, grabbing for Benny, but Aiken had grown fat and Benny was still in the prime of youth.

"What the…" Aiken stammered.

"You gotta get going if you expect to make it back from Down Mountain before tomorrow morn."

"Ah, bullocks! Have Jack get it himself," He stumbled over to the bed, fell face first onto the fur blankets and passed out cold.

"Aiken? Aiken, WAKE UP!" Benny screamed.

He shook his brother with all his might, but all he got was the same drunken babble.

"To hell with you then!"

Benny changed his clothes, drew some more water to wash his face and walked back to Jack's place. Jack was the only real friend Benny had, and Jack knew how Aiken was, which is why he always kept some coins aside to give to Benny when the drunkard spent it all.

Benny found the Den deserted except for Liverwart, carrying two drunken dwarves over his shoulders. He was only around 8 feet tall, short for a giant, and he could barely fit in the dining hall, but he was always handy when it came to carrying bodies. Throwing them down hard onto the cobblestone path, he turned to Benny. Upon seeing the young lad, he waved a huge, wart covered hand and wobbled over.

"Me glad *um* see you."

He pushed his bushy brown hair out of his face and smiled down at Benny. Liverwart could understand the common tongue perfectly, but he could barely speak it; usually mixing it in with his own tribal dialect.

"Yeah, same here. Where's Jack?" Benny asked, eager to walk away.

"*Mun um…*Jack gone."

"Where'd he go?"

"*Um dum.*" The giant stated.

"Well, that's a great help." Benny said.

The barmaid, Nadia, was busy rearranging the tables and weaving between equally large puddles of urine and vomit. A single man wearing a dirty coif lay rolled up in a ball in the corner, hiccupping.

"Where'd Jack go?" Benny asked.

"I dunno. Somewhere with those fellas from last night." she replied.

"Beranger and Cycleze?"

"Dale and the other, the funny dressed one."

"That's them all right," he said. Then he picked up on something else. "Dale?"

"Dale Beranger, Jack's friend."

His mind was racing. Dale? The hideous hulk was Dale? The one that Nadia liked? How could that be?

"Don't look so astonished. Dale's a real man. That's what counts."

"I guess you judge by more than looks," he said weakly.

He sat down in the seat where the two had been sitting last night, looking behind him at the cheery faces of the gnomes painted on the wall. The blue one was hanging upside down on a tree limb, seemingly winking at Benny.

"Aiken go to pick up the stuff?" Nadia asked, changing the subject.

"No."

She shrugged in indifference and walked away.

He walked across the river, all two feet of it, and went to sleep in the spare room Jack kept reserved in case Benny couldn't go home. He slept soundly through the day and into the night until he heard his name being called from outside.

"What?" Benny yelled at the unknown voice.

"It's Jack. Can I come in?"

Without waiting for an answer, Jack entered the room, grinning like a fool. He sat down on the edge of the bed and slapped Benny's leg.

"Aiken was passed out at home. I came to tell you he wasn't going to Down Mountain, but you were gone." Benny said, not bothering to sit up.

"I figured as much and went with Dale and Cyc to pick the stuff up myself. Wouldn't you know they were delivering some furs to some traders in Down Mountain? Ha ha! They gave me a ride and even loaned me their wagon to get back. Good ol' boys, they are."

"They're downright loony," Benny retorted. And so was Nadia, maybe.

"Ah, they've just had a rougher life than most people. Dale has anyway. Don't know too much about the other fella. He never talks."

Benny sat up finally and opened the shutters on his window.

"Where do you know them from?" Benny asked.

"Back when I lived in Alsbury, before moving to Gant to take over the inn when my father retired. You know the place, don't you?" Jack asked.

"Yeah, where those orcs massacred the children at the orphanage, right?"

"Yes! It was right around that time that I met Dale. You see, Dale's brother had been killed by an orc tribe that lived on the border of the town, and so he tried to gather a party to go snuff 'em out, but the town didn't want any part of it."

"So what'd he do?" Benny asked.

"He couldn't do nothing, the town wouldn't let 'em. He tried to warn them that something bad was gonna happen if those orcs weren't taken care of, but nobody listened. That's when the massacre happened. You see, about a mile south of the town was this big orphanage with dozens of children. Now, some orcs had been spotted hunting near the place, and Dale heard about it and tried to warn everyone before more innocent people died at the hands of those monsters. I believed him, but nobody else did and…well… Dale finally figured he'd go and check things out himself and stake the place out, and when he got there…" Jack stopped for a minute and shuddered.

"What?" Benny leaned forward, eager to hear the story through, "What happened?"

"What'd you think? The orcs had killed every last child! They'd filleted them alive, and had done all kinds of vulgar, carnal things with their bodies…some kind of ritual. Some orcs were still there, and Dale was so infuriated he tried to take on a dozen or so single handedly. That's how he got that scar."

"What happened then?" Benny was on the edge of the bed.

"Well, he made it back to Alsbury with his face torn to bits, and he told us what happened. Needless to say, the town finally rallied together, and we went and killed those orcs! Dale even managed to get up enough strength to lead the charge; poor sap just strapped a piece of cloth around his face and led us into the woods past that orphanage. We came upon those rotten orcs in their sleep and killed every man, woman, and child of 'em!"

Jack gave a proud laugh and slapped his own knee before his face returned to that of shame and regret.

'If only we'd acted sooner…anyway, after that, the town dubbed Dale the 'Avenger of Alsbury!' A title befitting! You should have seen 'em, Ben. That man killed over 20 orcs single handedly, and with his face falling apart to boot!"

Benny knew if Jack said he'd been in Alsbury when this occurred, Jack was telling the truth. Taking the story to heart, Benny realized he'd been too hasty in judging the man. He was still suspicious about the other one, though.

"What about his partner? " Benny asked.

"Who, Cyc? I dunno. He came into town shortly before the killings. Didn't talk much even then, but he and Dale seemed to hit it off. Come to think of it, after Dale went to check out the orphanage, Cyc went along after him to help. I think he chased off the orcs and helped him back to Alsbury. You know, my memory ain't what it used to be… anyway, after Dale got healed up the three of us did a lot of traveling, doing odd jobs here and there, until my father asked me to take over the Fox Den in Gant. It was then I decided to settle down and live out my life in peace."

"Well, if that's all true, I guess they aren't all bad."

"No! Benny, Dale may act rough and tumble, but that man is one of the best there has ever been!" Jack stood up and walked to the door before looking back at Benny. "But if he ever passes through here again, don't tell 'em I told you what happened. He doesn't like bringing up the past."

CHAPTER 3

Aiken ran off the next night, taking what little coin he'd had hidden in the house, and stole the blacksmith's horse. Benny wasn't too concerned with it, and was actually glad to be rid of him. He grabbed what few clothes, books, and trinkets he had and moved into the room at the Fox Den. It was clean and cozy, and aside from helping out with some chores every now and then, Jack let Benny do as he pleased. The weeks passed uneventfully, outside of the occasional brawls between humans and the dwarves that passed through on their way home from the mines. Liverwart usually broke up the fights. On one night, the giant even threw a particularly obnoxious patron through the window and into the river. Needless to say, Jack wasn't too pleased.

"You dunderheaded idiot! I said stop the fight, not tear the building down!" Jack was poking Liverwart in the stomach with his finger, and the giant stood looking into the air, proud and apathetic with his arms crossed on his chest.

"I try pull apart, he *num* hit me," the giant replied.

"Well, he ain't gonna pay to replace my window, and you certainly won't, will you?" Jack asked. "I don't think so!"

The giant pushed Jack aside, sending him crashing into a

crowd of men playing dice at a table. Jack's face was that of pure rage, but he knew the giant could kill him in one blow. He let Liverwart stomp out of the dining hall, crushing one of the wooden steps on the porch in the process.

"Can anyone do what I ask around here?" Jack threw his hands up in the air and sat down in an unoccupied stool.

"It's probably because you don't pay him enough," yelled Nap in the background, stopping a song mid-verse.

"Well, that's the third time that dumb giant has wrecked my establishment. He's supposed to be my bouncer. He can stop a problem in a hurry, but sooner or later he's going to destroy the place."

"Well, get someone else to be the bouncer," said Nadia, "We got plenty of tough guys around here ready to bash heads if trouble starts."

Benny heard the door slam open and turned. His gaze was immediately drawn to the gaping nostrils in Dale Beranger's face. There was a loud yelp from Nap at the other end of the room; he quickly disappeared from sight.

"What's this I hear about trouble?" Beranger asked.

Jack threw his hands in the air but said nothing.

"Well whatever it is, I'm sure it's nothing a few pints can't fix. Bring us a round!" He hobbled bow legged towards Jack's table, pushing a patron out of his chair and commandeering it.

"Hey!" the man shouted.

"Hay's for horses," Beranger replied. The man shook himself off and moved to another chair.

"I feel so stupid," Jack finally said.

"See, you're finally being honest with yourself!" Beranger slapped Jack on the shoulder, sending him lurching forward.

"Don't start, Dale."

"Oh, shove off! Where's your infamous sense of humor?"

"It just stormed out the building, or did you miss it?" Jack replied.

"What? That big buffoon? I can take him out of commission if you'd like…"

Beranger stood up and began to grab for the small metal rod he had stuck in his belt, but when Jack saw him reaching for it he grabbed Beranger's wrist.

"No! No! No! No Violence!"

"But violence feels so good!" Beranger laughed.

He held out the rod, and out of nowhere it transformed into a club almost 5 feet long, and with a flick of his wrist, dozens of steel spikes several inches long popped out over the entire length of it. He slammed it down on the table where the men were gambling and ripped up a huge portion of the table. Beranger cackled like a banshee.

"What the hell!" Jack yelled, jumping to his feet.

"You like?" Beranger asked, flicking his wrist again, causing the club to transform back into the harmless steel rod, "A gift from one of my many travels…centuries old! You can't find weapons like this anymore."

"Well, you're gonna need more than that if you keep destroying my property!"

Beranger pulled a hefty sack off his belt and shook it in front of Jack's face. Benny heard the clinking of coins, and his mouth dropped to the floor as the lunatic poured over a dozen gold coins onto the floor at Jack's feet.

"How about that?" Beranger snapped.

"Yeah… that's better."

Beranger turned to Benny and winked.

"He still working you like a slave driver?" he asked.

"You guessed it." Benny was trying his best not to appear nervous. Was it for his money that Nadia liked this man?

"How'd you get back here so fast anyway?" Jack asked while frantically picking up gold from the floor, "I didn't think you'd be passing back through here for quite some time."

"I have a little proposition for you." Beranger said.

"Oh no you don't! I'm way too old to go prancing around the country with you!"

"Dear God! I never thought I'd see the day!" Beranger chuckled.

"We almost got killed half a dozen times! Hunting vampires, slaying goblin hoards, raiding ships on the coast, and countless other episodes…I've retired! I can barely keep this place from crumbling around me!"

"What exactly do you do?" Nadia asked Beranger, looking skeptical. But now Benny could see that there was a certain diffidence about her. She was trying to impress the man, but it didn't seem to be working.

"Anything and everything. There's not really a title for my…" he pointed to Jack, "…our profession. Monster hunting, body guarding, mercenary work, delivery and retrieval…even assassinations if the price is right. "

"Assassinations?! You're joking about that last part, right?" Benny asked. Jack's faced flushed a deep scarlet of embarrassment, and he attempted to sputter out a reply to his young friend until Beranger cut in.

"Don't worry your little head, baby boy. Mostly just escaped prisoners doomed for the gallows anyway."

"You promised you wouldn't tell 'em about *that* part…"

Jack buried his face into his hands in shame. Nadia, eager to leave the awkward conversation, made up some excuse about checking to make sure the rooms were clean for some patrons and scurried off. Despite the roar of voices within the dining hall, there was an eerie silence among the three. Then, without even thinking, Benny made a request that he at first thought had come from someone else.

"I could go with you." Now what was he thinking of? Was he trying to get the measure of the man Nadia liked?

Jack looked up, surprised, and Beranger gave a snaggletooth grin. *Did I just say that?!* Benny thought. A lump formed at the back of his throat, and it was beginning to get hard for him to swallow. He was regretting his statement already.

"No!" cried Jack. "No! Absolutely not! You've never even left Gant before, Ben! What makes you think you can keep up with this guy?" He was furious.

"Laughing Jack, you cut me to the quick," Beranger said. "You know I'll look after him, and besides, the boy's big enough to do a bit of exploring on his own. The boy's grown his pubes, hasn't he? It's not like we're tackling bat monsters in the Bletian Caverns. We just gotta deliver a package." He winked at Benny again.

"Oh, really? And what kind of package is that?" Jack inquired.

"Sorry, lad. It's confidential." He slugged Jack on the shoulder and chuckled again.

"Well, I'm telling you, Ben, it ain't a good idea. Not that I don't trust Dale here, but I can't…"

Benny cut in again, speaking against his own urge not to. His voice didn't even sound like his own. "You can't what? You're not my father or my brother. You can't make decisions for me, Jack. Everyone else my age has already left home. Aiken was the only reason I stayed around, and he's gone now. Come on, Jack! It's not like I'll be gone forever; Beranger said himself it's only one little job. We'll be back before you know it, right?" Benny turned a pleading look to Beranger.

"Yeah, Jack. We'll be back before you know it," Beranger said, his whiny voice mocking Benny's.

"Well, Ben, I guess you're a grown lad; you can do as you please." Jack stood up and walked back to the kitchen. He was obviously hurt. Benny's guilt was already bringing tears to his eyes. He didn't know why he'd said he wanted to go with Beranger; in all honesty he didn't want to. But in some strange way, which he couldn't explain, he felt compelled to join the scar-faced man in his journeys, regardless of what hells awaited them. Had he turned towards the window behind him, he would have noticed the figure of Cycleze, watching his every move while muttering strange incantations.

Chapter 4

Benny must've stood in front of Jack's door for half an hour that night before gathering the courage to knock. He heard a faint 'come in' and slowly opened the door. Jack was sitting at the far end of his room on the third floor, reading a scrap of parchment under dim candlelight. He turned and saw Benny standing in the doorway, his silhouette marked by moonlight. He smiled half-heartedly and bid Benny to come in.

"Jack, I…"

"No, Ben, it's okay." Jack turned towards him, "you're right. You need to get out and experience the world a bit. I trust Dale, and rowdy as he may be, he'll keep you out of trouble." He chuckled. "Better you than Nadia."

"Nadia!"

"She has a crush on him, same as you do on her. But he's got no use for her. None that she'd put up with, anyway. Best to keep her close to home."

Benny wanted to tell Jack that he was sorry, and that he didn't know what he was doing when he said he wanted to go with Beranger and Cycleze, but as before he couldn't bring himself to say it.

"Here; I pulled out my old traveling gear. Try it on." Jack set out a traveling bag filled to the brim with clothes. Benny tried to put on a cheerful face and began putting on a thick burgundy tunic and some tan leggings. The clothes were a bit baggy on his 16-year-old frame, and the steel plated boots seemed unnecessary for long travels, but Jack insisted that the feet were a vital body part to be protected.

"If the going gets tough, your feet need to be safe before anything else. Heavy body armor will weigh you down, but if them puppies take one good blow, you're immovable…might as well throw yourself on your own sword at that point." Jack stated.

"But, if that's the case, they ain't gonna do me any good. I can barely walk as it is," Benny replied.

"Oh, you'll get used to that before you know it. Trust me. And since you mentioned swords…" Jack pulled out an old sword from under his bed. It was sheathed and already attached to a cracked leather belt. He pulled it out to reveal an old steel blade, notched on both sides with jagged teeth, a number of which were broken off.

"I thought those were illegal in Dan since the wars?" Benny asked.

"They are…if they catch you using it. Just don't go pulling it out for show and tell and you'll be fine. Those Galver Dorn rangers are hardly ever patrolling Dan anyways." He handed it to Benny and the boy strapped it on. "Now, let's take a look."

He pulled Benny in front of a mirror so Benny could view his wardrobe. His face was pale and flushed with rosiness as usual, giving him a very feminine look, which he disliked. His hair was almost the same white-blond that Beranger's had been, but was much longer and braided into a ponytail that hung down his back. The tunic was so loose that it hung off his right shoulder, and the weight of the sword pulled Benny's pants down on the right. He looked outright ridiculous, but Laughing Jack Baldwin was as proud as any wannabe parent could be, his bald head glistening in the candlelight, and his mouth stretched from ear to ear under his heavy mustache as he grinned.

"I do say, you're ready to conquer the world! But I will need that stuff back when you return." He turned back to his desk and began reading the same parchment as before.

"Will you see us off in the morning?" Benny asked.

Jack merely nodded, and Benny left the room, returning to his own.

CHAPTER 5

The next morning came quicker then Benny expected, and after an entire night of not being able to sleep, he was even more skeptical about the journey ahead of him. Beranger and Cycleze were ready and waiting for him, having reoccupied the wagon Jack had borrowed a few weeks prior, empty except for a burlap sack that was stained a dark brown color at the bottom; it buzzed with flies. The duo sat in the front seat saying their goodbyes to Jack, who was repairing the steps Liverwart destroyed the night before.

"Rise and shine, pudding cup!" Beranger yelled as he spotted Benny, "You can ride up here with us. I'd say sit in the wagon, but there's a package stewing back there."

"I'm not even gonna ask..." said Jack with a chuckle. He gave a cheerful smile at Benny, but it was obvious he wasn't glad to see the boy leave. Benny looked again at the suspicious sack, but decided it was best to ignore it; it was their business.

"Now, I'm serious, Dale! No funny stuff! Take the boy around Dan, show him some of the sites, teach him to swing that ol' sword a bit and bring him back," Jack was pointing his finger repeatedly at the duo. Beranger laughed while Cycleze looked forward, his chest heaving with silent laughter.

"Jack, when have I ever gotten anyone in any trouble? You treat us like a couple of vagabonds!" He nodded for Benny to hop onto the seat.

"Look out for him, Cyc." Jack yelled to the bearded man. They both nodded at each other, as if sharing some unknown agreement.

Benny waved goodbye to Jack one final time, and shouted a farewell to Nadia and Nap, who'd barreled out of the front door just in time to wave goodbye as well. Nap took one step too far and fell face first into the horse trough. Benny chuckled and turned around in his seat, staring at the mule, which was transporting them out of Gant.

"We're gonna have to do something about that hair, boy," Beranger spoke. "We got a lot of open road and camping ahead of us. Those locks and soft facial features might give a man some ideas!"

He cackled like a banshee, and Cycleze's chest heaved again as he laughed without noise. He looked down at Benny and shrugged, as if saying *he doesn't mean anything by it*.

"I'm not a queer!" Benny retorted. Beranger began laughing even harder.

"Then stop looking like one!"

Most of their travel consisted of long, obscene rants by Beranger, usually directed at Benny. They traveled through the mountain paths, stopping at night and sleeping off the road. Benny quickly saw how paranoid Beranger was, because every night Beranger and Cycleze would rotate every two hours to stand watch for anything creeping up on them. This perhaps wasn't a big thing when camping in the wild, but from what he already knew about Beranger, he wouldn't doubt that the duo had made enemies during their travels. The forested mountains slowly dropped into more level terrain, and soon the forests thinned out into grassy plains. The temperature grew from a mountain chill to a scorching midday heat as the wagon rattled along. All the three ate and drank were water, beef jerky Jack had given them, and whatever animals Beranger felt like killing at night. One morning, when they were getting ready to go, Benny's curiosity finally caused him to peek in the bag that sat in the wagon bed. There was a putrid smell Benny had never encountered before, and as he undid the string around the bag, the morning sun beamed down on a severed human head: green and bloated, with the hair falling out and blisters formed on the skin. The face was contorted in a horrifying scream that decomposition had only worsened. Benny immediately dropped the bag, lurched over and began to puke. Beranger stopped adjusting the mule's harness and a look of annoyance crossed his face.

"Shit! He looked, Cycleze. He had to look!" He threw his hands up and chuckled sarcastically. Still bent over, with vomit stringing from his lips, Benny looked at Beranger.

"It's a…it's a…" Benny stuttered.

"A head," a croaking voice said from behind him. Benny turned around to see Cycleze, arms crossed on his chest and standing still as a statue. Those were the first words the man had spoken since Benny met him.

"Don't act all shocked, Benny my boy. You knew about the work I do, and like I said," He reached into the wagon and retied the top of the bag. "He was just an escaped fugitive."

Benny said nothing the rest of the trip; the image of the bloated, discolored, contorted face haunted his ever-waking thought. In the far distance, Benny could see the beginning of another forest, although not nearly as thick as in Gant. Soon they were deep in a pine grove, and not long after that they came upon a small village. It wasn't nearly as large as Gant; the Fox Den would dwarf the largest building. This barn-like building was on stilts, with stairs in front leading up to a loft area where Benny could see a table and several men dressed in furs, hovering over a portly man looking at something Benny couldn't see. Beranger stopped the cart in front of the building.

"Is Tak Larson here?" he asked a small boy sitting on top of an old barrel. The boy pointed up to the loft but said nothing.

"Stay here...I have a gift for Tak," he grabbed the sack containing the unidentified head and marched up the stairs.

"Who's Tak?" Benny asked Cycleze.

The man said nothing. Benny looked back up at the loft, but at this close he couldn't see anyone. He heard a thump followed by the surprised yelps of several men. One voice, louder than the others, chastised Beranger both for interrupting a meeting as well for dropping a human head onto plans for a community hall. There was some more talking followed by a loud crashing noise, more screaming, and a demand by Beranger.

"Live up to your word!" he shouted.

Benny ran up the stairs, not stopping to think. When he got to the top, everyone turned to look at the boy. Beranger had his spiked club at the portly man's neck. Two men had fallen back on the floor, the table was smashed in half, and one frail man stood in a defensive posture, half-heartedly holding a short sword in front of him.

"Go away, Ben." Beranger said.

"Um…okay." Benny replied.

When Beranger finally walked back down the stairs, his club was transformed back into the small metal rod, and in the other hand he held a hefty bag of coins. He winked at both of his companions and climbed back into the wagon seat.

"He got pissy because I interrupted some meeting. Didn't want to pay the bounty…said I was supposed to take care of business in private. He paid up though." He chuckled.

"Beranger? Dale Beranger?" A young elf dressed in a white messenger's cloak called out, standing in the middle of the encampment.

"What the hell do you want?!" Beranger yelled.

The elf ran swiftly over to Beranger and gave him a slip of parchment. He read it, laughed out loud, and threw it back at the messenger. The elf gave an annoyed look, turned, and before Benny could see where he went, sprinted out of the camp.

"Who was that?" Benny asked.

"An elf messengers from Galver Dorn. Looks like Duke Dijon has a job for us," he said.

CHAPTER 6

They were on the way to Galver Dorn, the wagon now trundling through mixed oak and pine forests. Benny found it interesting because he had not been this far from Gant before, but the men were plainly bored.

"Do you want to take the reins for a while, lad?" Beranger inquired. "You might as well get in some practice for when you take the wagon back to Jack. We won't need it after this next mission."

Benny jumped, thinking he was dreaming. Why was Beranger acting so civil all of a sudden? "Uh--" he said, mentally flailing.

Both men laughed. "I'm not always a belligerent hick," Beranger said. "When dealing with these inbred country yokels, you have to act like one. Always bring yourself to the same level as those you interact with. You'll know their way of thinking, how you should conduct yourself, and how you can control the outcome of any situation. Understand?"

"Sure…it makes sense," Benny said, "despite being a little offended by the 'inbred yokel' remark."

"So how about the reins? My arms are getting tired."

"Sure, I can take the reins, if you wish. As long as I

know where to go."

"There are several trails; they all lead to Galver Dorn from here. Pick the one you like, but stay out of sight when you can. We don't like dealing with strangers. Meanwhile, Cycleze and I will nap."

They trusted him enough to choose the route? "All right," Benny agreed uncertainly. Something didn't smell quite right about this, but he couldn't place the problem. Certainly he could alert the others if any question arose. Were they testing him? He did know how to guide a horse.

He moved up and took the reins. The others flopped down in the bed of the wagon and were soon asleep.

Now that he was on his own, as it were, Benny found himself thinking about Nadia. He was satisfied that she had no interest in him; no girl did. But how could she have a thing for Beranger, who was crude, ugly, and a bully? Did muscle and money make that much of a difference? It was clear that Jack knew about it, and seemed not to fully approve though he called Beranger his friend. Maybe it was that being on the trail with a pair of ruffians was no place for a pretty girl. Benny had no illusions about the kind of duty she would have to serve out here; any unprotected woman who did not submit voluntarily got raped. So it seemed she needed Jack's protection from rough men and from her own odd inclination for this one.

In the afternoon, the men still snoring, they came to a three-way fork in the road. One was the broad main route that the wagon tracks showed was what most folk used. Another was a thin winding trail suitable only for travelers on foot. The third was just wide enough for the wagon. That was surely the road less traveled by, the kind that Beranger preferred. It looked nice enough.

Except for one thing: there was a crude sign marking it with an X. That meant it was not supposed to be used. Why? All trails were public; no one had the right to reserve one for his own use. All these trails went to the same place, ultimately; he could not get lost. Still, warnings were not lightly ignored.

Benny considered. What would Beranger say? He'd say take it and damn the presumptuous idiot who posted the sign. Signs were only as legitimate as the folk who made and enforced them. On to Galver Dorn. So Benny steered the horse to that one.

It turned out to be a good trail, level and firm. The trees pressed in closely but not too closely. Benny was glad he had taken it.

There was a roar ahead. Uh-oh; Benny didn't like the sound of that. But the trail was too narrow for them to turn, and backing up would be complicated; it wasn't *that* smooth. There was nothing to do but proceed forward, and hope the roar related to something else.

Then the ground shook with the measured tramping of giant steps. Too late Benny realized his folly: he had taken a trail reserved by a mountain giant! There would be hell to pay.

He glanced back into the wagon. Beranger and Cycleze remained sound asleep, not bothered at all by the bouncing of the wagon, the shaking of the ground, or the roars of the giant. That was amazing.

Then he caught on: they were faking it. This was a sort of initiation, to see how well he handled a crisis on his own.

He was not doing well, so far. He had gotten them into what could be real trouble, and had almost no idea how to get them out. He needed to admit it, and give them time to get clear of the wagon before the giant demolished it. This disaster was on his head.

Yet something in him refused to yield to the obvious need. He was desperate to redeem himself if he possibly could. What could he do?

The giant did not wait on his deliberation. A ten-foot tall monster man exploded into sight on the trail ahead. He was naked, with grotesquely bulging muscles and huge warts on his hands and feet. "Ho!" the giant exclaimed with violent satisfaction.

"Uh, ho," Benny said. If the giant was similar to Liverwart, he would be able to understand normal human dialect well, but be crude in speaking it. "Nice trail you have here. You take good care of it."

The giant stomped to a halt before the horse. "You got food?"

"Not really," Benny said. The wagon could have been piled high with food, yet barely feed this monster. As it was, their supplies were meager; they needed more.

"Treasure?"

"No." What use would a giant have for riches?

"Girls?"

"No." As if any human women could survive the savage lust of the giant.

"Then what you bring for ransom?"

"Nothing," Benny said. "We're just passing through. It's really a public trail, isn't it?"

"Me trail."

"No, not according to the law of the land. Nobody owns a public trail." This wasn't going well.

"Me trail," the giant repeated with certainty.

Benny tried another ploy. "Hello. I am Benny from

Gant. Who are you?"

"Me Kidneywart."

"Ah, I know Liverwart! Are you related?"

"Shrimp me cousin. Weakling."

So much for that. "Well, nice to meet you, Kidneywart. We'll be moving on now."

"Plunder?"

"No plunder," Benny said firmly. "Now if you will just step aside, please."

"Then me eat you. And horse."

"Oh, I wouldn't advise that," Benny said, alarmed.

"Me dawdle long enough. Me hungry." Kidneywart reached suddenly forward across the length of the horse and caught Benny about the waist. He heaved him up from the wagon seat and brought him to his out-sized face. He opened his mouth to expose an array of teeth like those of a horse. Benny was helpless.

"One moment, if you please," a voice behind Benny said.

The giant peered beyond him. "Who you?"

"I am Dale Beranger, traveler and warrior. Now I am asking you nicely: put down that youth, pigface, and get your sorry butt out of our way before I get annoyed."

"Me eat you next, man thing," Kidneywart decided. He lifted Benny back up toward his gaping orifice.

"I strongly recommend that you be reasonable, basilisk breath," Beranger said evenly. "My patience has limits."

The giant put Benny into his mouth, about to bite off his head, literally. Then suddenly he flung Benny away. "Oww!"

Benny dropped to the ground and scrambled to his feet, bruised but intact. He saw the giant doubling over in

33

pain. Beranger, now standing beside the horse, had struck one of his feet with his spiked club. Blood was gushing from the wound.

"Oh, have I got your attention now, sawdust brain?" Beranger asked. "Then please allow me to speak more plainly: get your horse ass out of my way before I am forced to chastise you, frog mouth."

If the giant was annoyed before, that was over. Now he was enraged. A tree-trunk sized club appeared in his ham-like hand. "Me pull ize you!" He lifted his weapon high.

"Did you by any chance mean to say 'pulverize'?" Beranger inquired. "You should learn to speak more plainly, piss nose." Then he spiked the giant's other foot.

Benny, amazed, glanced at Cycleze, who was now seated on the edge of the wagon. He was surprised to see the man not only unafraid, but smiling slightly as if amused.

"Oww!" Kidneywart repeated, doubling over again.

This time Beranger clubbed his head, which was now in reach. The spike smashed into one eye and stabbed deep into the brain behind it. It was a killing blow. The giant toppled to the side, landing beside the trail with a crash.

"You did warn him," Cycleze said. "Politely."

Beranger shrugged as he wiped off his stained club. "He did not listen well."

Then the two men drew their knives and set about carving large steaks from the giant's body. Now they had plenty of food stored.

Benny faced into the forest and vomited.

In due course they resumed their trek. "I—I'm sorry I got us into that mess," Benny said. "So that you had to bail me out."

Cycleze laughed. "We wanted the meat."

Benny stared at him. "You—you and Dale *wanted* me to steer into the giant's territory?"

"Sure," Beranger said. "We'd have had trouble running him down if we chased him. But he figured you were safe prey."

This was hardly complimentary to Benny, but he stifled that thought. For one thing, he now knew that the very last person he ever wanted to run afoul of was Beranger. That man had proven what a deadly fighter he was.

"So you were testing me," he said. "Giving me my head, to see what I'd do."

"That's right," Beranger said affably. "And you did what you were told to. And you tried to handle it yourself. Not your fault that you haven't yet learned how to fight a giant. We'll teach you that in good time."

"Thank you." That would have been ironic, were it not something he realized that he really did need to learn. "There must be other things I need to pick up on."

"Dozens," Beranger agreed. "Keep your eyes open, see how we operate. You'll get there in due course."

That would be good. If he didn't get himself killed first.

CHAPTER 7

They camped the night in Kidneywart Giant's massive
stronghold, which was a structure formed of braided
saplings with a bone stairway to a second floor and sod for
a roof. It was comfortable enough, and reasonably weather-
tight. There was a parlor containing hanging scorched
carcasses and a fair amount of grain, right next to the open
trench latrine. Evidently the giant had not been scrupulous
about hygiene.

"Feed the horse," Beranger told Benny, indicating the
grain with a thumb. "We want to keep him in fine fettle for
Jack." Benny fetched a metal pan, filled it with grain, and
took it out to the horse. There was also a water trough so
the animal could drink.

"Now where is it?" Beranger mused.

Benny decided not to ask what the man was looking
for, fearing he would not like the answer.

"There'll be a pit," Cycleze said.

"Ah, so," Beranger agreed. He scuffed the dirt floor
with one boot, and soon found a metallic disk with a stout
ring in its center. He pulled on the ring, but it didn't budge.

"A hand here," he snapped at Benny.

Benny joined him, and together they managed to heave the heavy lid up. Below was a dark hole. Had it really been too much for Beranger to do alone, or was he simply getting Benny involved? Did it matter?

"Torch."

Benny took a torch from a crude holder in the main chamber. It smelled of swamp gas. Beranger brought out a flint and struck a spark, igniting the torch as Benny held it up. The flame was smoky, but it did provide enough light to illuminate the chamber.

"Get down there," Beranger said.

Benny obeyed. He climbed carefully into the dark void, holding the torch aloft. Below was a dank mud cave lined with what looked like drawers. He pulled on one, and it slid out of its recess: a solid wood box. He lifted the lid. It was filled with sparkling jewelry and golden coins evidently taken from Kidneywart's victims. This was the giant's treasure!

"Hand it up."

Benny propped the torch awkwardly against the side of the heavy box and hoisted it up so that the man could take it.

"Tourist junk," Beranger said, disgusted. "Fake gold trinkets, false pearls, glass gems, polished brass coins. The idiot thought anything that sparkled was valuable. Put it back."

Benny took the box and shoved it back in its hole. He had been fooled too.

"You worked at the inn, boy," Beranger said. "You know what to do."

Benny did. They closed off the cellar, then Benny ground some of the grain in the giant's huge mortar and pestle and used the flour to make crude pancakes for dinner, cooked on the out-sized grill. It wasn't nearly as good as what

Laughing Jack or Nadia routinely made, but it sufficed. The men ate them without comment, evidently not expecting anything better.

They slept on the second floor platform. "Want to take your turn?" Beranger asked.

He had a choice? "Yes." Benny was determined to pull his weight.

"First shift." The other two flopped down and were immediately asleep, or emulating it, despite the hours they had spent snoring in the wagon. Benny sat up, gazing around and listening. After a few minutes the snoring stopped; they were no longer faking it. But they would surely wake instantly if there were any reason to. That business with the giant proved that; Beranger had been more than ready when the time came.

The giant. Now that he had quiet time, Benny pondered that. Yes, Kidneywart had been a rough brute who preyed on travelers and ate people, literally. But Benny had steered into his lair despite the posted warning. The giant had played fair, letting travelers know the danger; they could readily have avoided it. So while Benny didn't like Kidneywart, he really could not blame him for being what he was. Had it been right to kill him? True, little short of that would have saved Benny's life, once he had blundered into that trap. He did owe Beranger his life. So it was better not to question the man's decisions.

Beranger: he was rough and tough, all right, but his abilities had to be respected. Interesting that he tolerated Benny's presence, knowing that Benny had joined them on a foolish whim.

And what of Nadia? Was she justified in hankering for Beranger despite his appearance? Women liked men of power, just as men liked women of beauty; such combinations were standard in marriage. Maybe it showed that she was at heart sensible.

And finally himself: why had he done it? Abruptly deciding to join the adventurers, instead of staying safely home or at the inn? When trouble came, he had never even thought to try to use the fine old sword Jack had given him. Some warrior he was! He was not at all cut out for this rough life. Yet here he was. He could make no real sense of any of this, least of all his own place in it.

Cycleze stirred, stretched, and sat up. "My turn," he said.

Had his shift passed already? Benny realized that hours had passed while he pondered. So he didn't argue. He lay down and soon slept, satisfied that he had done his part.

In the morning they woke, pissed, pooped, washed, and ate more pancakes. They closed up the stronghold; soon enough another giant would discover it and make it his own. Then they were on their way again.

The giant's trail intersected the main road, and that led to the town of Galver Dorn. It was larger than Gant, with many outlying fields, orchards, and huts. It had a more civilized look. Benny realized that he had grown up in the hinterland, out of touch with the larger world.

Beranger took over the reins and guided them to a meat wholesaler on the edge of town. "Got a fresh load of meat for you, harvested yesterday," he told the attendant.

"What kind?" the man asked.

"Giant."

The man laughed. Then Beranger lifted the canvas cover. The man stopped laughing. "Oh."

"It's good meat, and cheap," Beranger said. "You don't

need to advertise where it came from. It'll be just as good in stew and meat pies and to feed the dogs."

"Uh, yes," the man agreed. They bargained for a price, and hands unloaded the wagon and hosed it off to clear most of the blood.

Benny was relieved that they hadn't actually eaten any of it themselves.

Duke Dijon resided in a downtown multistory building. Benny tried to conceal his amazement at his first experience with either downtown—villages lacked them—and many-floored buildings, ditto. The Fox Den Inn was the only one he had known with a third story. He really was a country boy.

Dijon was a portly bald man in a dark suit. If he was really a duke he didn't show it, but there was an air of authority about him. He greeted Beranger like an old friend, as perhaps he was. It was clear that Beranger had many obscure connections. "We have two situations, each dire in its own way. We really need your help," he said. He didn't ask who Beranger's companions were; maybe he preferred not to know.

Beranger got to the point. "We'll take them one at a time. What's the fee?"

"One pound bag of gold." He presented the bag.

"Per situation," Beranger said.

Dijon opened his mouth to protest, then reconsidered. "You always were a hard bargainer."

Beranger took the bag, opened it, and dumped it out on the table, making a small pile of bright gold coins. He carefully bit each coin, verifying its nature. "This is no ordinary mission," he said. "You could buy a small army for this."

"That's right. No ordinary man will tackle it, and no

army either, but the need is desperate. I'm depending on you. You have a way of accomplishing things."

"You can depend on me," Beranger agreed. "But before I take this money, I need to know what it's for. I'm not into political assassination: too many legal complications."

"No politics," Dijon agreed. "Zombies."

"Shit!" Beranger swore. "I don't like zombies."

"Nobody does," Dijon said evenly. "That's why this is a problem."

Beranger looked at him. Then he looked at the gold. "I should have known it would be something like this."

"Will you do it?"

Beranger looked at Cycleze. Cycleze shrugged.

Beranger looked at Benny. "Uh, I don't know anything about zombies," Benny said. "Except that I prefer to stay far away from them."

"We'll do it," Beranger said, piling the coins back into the bag and putting it away. "Now you tell Benny here exactly what he needs to know."

Benny was startled, but Dijon didn't question this. Evidently he was used to Beranger's nuances. Maybe it was Beranger's way of not admitting that there were things he didn't know about zombies. "There are different kinds of zombies," he said. "They are all half dead, really animated corpses. They have no feeling of pain and are virtually mindless. Those who are freshly dead can seem almost alive, while those that have been dead for years can be walking tatters of rotten flesh. New ones can still see and hear, to a degree, and have fair coordination, but all that fades in days. Old ones lose their ears and eyeballs and can readily be avoided. Some keep largely to themselves; others go looking for human flesh to eat. Some will even do odd chores

41

in return for being tolerated, and females can have their clienteles though it's not safe to kiss them. It is important to know which kind you are dealing with. Do you understand?"

"Yes," Benny said with a shudder. "What kind must we deal with?"

"New ones, maybe three days old. That means they can be dangerous when they attack, despite going blind and their inoperative digestive systems."

"Why do they attack?"

Dijon smiled mirthlessly. "We don't exactly know what goes on in the so-called minds of zombies. But we conjecture that they vaguely know that they will soon enough rot away unless they get infusions of fresh living flesh. So they crave it. Their senses are degraded, but they know when living flesh is near, and go after it. That is the problem in our sister city of Elim Dorn: only about a quarter of the citizens were zombied, but those ones immediately went after the living ones, and will continue until all are consumed. So the population may now be down to half its original total, and diminishing daily. The citizens are too freaked out to fight back effectively. They need efficient leadership. Speed is of the essence."

"But how did that quarter get zombied in the first place?"

"Some background here: a wizard--" He paused. "Do you believe in magic?"

"Not really," Benny said.

"You'll get over that when you encounter it. The leading wizard of the city set up to craft a spell to cure a plague of flu they were experiencing. He's a good wizard, but he's getting old, and he made a mistake. He converted the flu virus to a zombie virus, and suddenly there were zombies in place of flu sufferers. So these are fresh ones, and there are many of them. They have to be promptly abolished, so that the damage spreads no further. The only way to abolish a zombie is to kill it, and that can be tricky."

"How can you kill something that's already dead?"

Dijon nodded. "How indeed! More correctly, you have to disable it, usually by pulling it apart and scattering the pieces, so that they can't function as a unit any more. It's a dirty business. They may twitch for weeks, but eventually they'll rot away. They can be dumped in a pit and left alone, and the pit can be sprayed to abate the odor."

"Yuk!"

"You will have proper tools, of course: protective over-clothes, waterproof boots, gauntlets, face masks. Swords. They are not actually contagious, even when they bite you; the flu was contagious, but when it became a zombie virus it infected only those already infected, if you appreciate what I mean. But it remains a challenge. If you receive enough zombie bites, you will die of trauma, or you could be smothered under piled bodies."

There was a pause. Then Beranger stood. "We'll take care of it."

"Then go and get outfitted. We wish you the best of success, and that is most sincere. We can't renovate Elim Dorn until it is entirely clear of zombies."

They departed the office without further word. Beranger knew where the outfitting store was, and before long the three of them were properly equipped. Theoretically they were ready, but Benny dreaded what was to come.

CHAPTER 8

It was afternoon as they rode the wagon on the road to Elim Dorn, with Beranger holding the reins. Now Cycleze spoke to Benny. "Two things for you, lad."

"Me?" Benny asked, startled because this was the first time the strange man had addressed him directly.

"First: why didn't the Duke throw a fit when we doubled the price?"

Benny hadn't thought of that. "I guess he knew it was pointless to argue terms with Dale."

Beranger let out a laugh that sounded almost like breaking wind.

"Try again, lad," Cycleze said.

So this was another test. Why was Cycleze doing it, instead of Beranger? That was a question for another day. "I guess he really wanted the jobs done, whatever the price, and knew he couldn't get anybody else."

"Closer," Beranger said, amused. "But your naivety could kill you."

"Don't miss it again, lad," Cycleze said, and there was something in his tone that made Benny shiver.

He struggled. This seemingly innocent question was not innocent at all. There was a deadly purpose behind it. Something he needed to figure out in a hurry. That his life could depend on. Not from any threat by the men, but by what he didn't understand. What could it be?

Then he got it: "Dijon thinks we won't survive the zombie mission! So what's the point arguing about what the second one will cost? He won't have to pay it anyway. He might even recover his gold from our dead bodies. With luck, we'll have taken out most of the zombies, reducing the problem for others."

Both men nodded. It seemed that Benny had learned proper cynicism for this kind of life. To understand hidden motives.

"And the second thing," Benny said. "We need to act to make sure we do survive it."

There was no response. That meant his answer was incomplete.

"And since I'm the weak spot in this team, you need to train me how to survive zombie combat. So I don't mess up and put you in unnecessary danger."

Both men nodded. He had passed.

They halted in a secluded glade in the forest, and let the horse graze while they practiced. Beranger scouted around and fetched three dead pine branches. "Here's your sword," he said, handing one to Benny. Cycleze took the third.

"We can't practice with our real weapons?" Benny asked. Then he corrected himself. "Because I'd be dead before I learned my mistake."

"The kid's got promise," Beranger remarked to Cycleze. "Okay, I'm a zombie. So's Cy. Fastest way to nullify me is to cut off my head so I can't see or hear."

45

"Or bite," Benny said with a shudder.

"Zombies do have a bit of brain, enough to enable them to orient on living prey. Failing that, cut off my arms so I can't grab you. Or my legs, so I can't chase you. Now for this practice, don't hit hard; we don't want to hurt each other."

"Not hard," Benny agreed nervously. He stepped away from Cycleze, suspecting that the man would rap him if he didn't, having been labeled a zombie. Cycleze nodded and did not pursue.

Beranger came at him, suddenly clumsy. He took wide, tottering steps and flailed his arms, seeming just about to fall over. It was almost comical, and Benny laughed.

Beranger's stick rapped against his shielded neck with a loud thwack! "You're dead," Beranger said.

Oops. There was nothing funny about a zombie, no matter how he walked.

They tried again. This time Benny blocked Beranger's deliberately clumsy blow and thwacked him neatly on the neck guard. Then he reconsidered. "Wait! Do Zombies use swords or sticks?"

Beranger threw away his stick. "They don't," he agreed. "But they do swing their arms, and bite."

They tried again. This time Benny struck Beranger's shoulder guard, theoretically cutting off the arm. The man staggered and fell against him. Suddenly his gaping mouth was in Benny's face. "You're dead," he said. "Don't let him clinch you, even one-armed. It's the teeth that will hurt you."

He was, of course, correct. Thereafter, Benny made sure not to let him get within touching range without losing his head, literally.

"You're catching on," Beranger said approvingly.

In due course they resumed travel. As evening closed

in, they came to the town of Elim Dorn. It looked much like Galver Dorn; there was no sign of mayhem. Maybe this was an undamaged section.

Cycleze paused to extend his arms up as if addressing some celestial deity. "The case is worse than we thought," he said after a moment. "There are few if any survivors. The town is lost."

He could tell that just by feeling the air?

"We'd better hole up in a house for the night," Beranger said. "One with a sealable stable; they eat horses, too."

"Did Dijon know?" Benny asked.

Both men nodded. "We're a suicide mission," Beranger said. "He thinks."

They drew up to an outlying cottage with an attached enclosed stable. Benny jumped down to check it out. A young woman came around the corner of the house, bare to the waist. She saw Benny and smiled, so glad to see a live man. She ran to embrace him, her face coming to meet his.

And dropped to the ground as Beranger's sword cut off her head.

"Hey!" Benny exclaimed, appalled. "She was alive!"

"No. Feel her," Beranger said. He caught Benny's hand and pressed it against the girl's back. It was clammy cold. Also, her severed neck was not bleeding, just oozing ichor. She was a zombie. "She was going to bite your face off."

"But she looked so real," Benny said. "She smiled when she saw me. She wasn't clumsy at all."

"These are very fresh zombies," Beranger said. "They still have all their flesh. The smile was her opening her mouth to take a bite. She ran like a zombie. You weren't looking at her legs."

It was true. Benny had been looking at her bare breasted

47

front. Now, he realized that a real live girl would not have exposed herself that way to a stranger. Zombies didn't care about clothing; they left it in place simply because they didn't notice it, and soon enough it fell away. And now he thought of it, her breasts had not bounced as live ones would; they had been fixed in place, maybe in a stage of rigor mortis.

"You're learning," Beranger said.

He was, indeed.

The house was empty. They entered it and found it to be in good order. The occupants must have fled when the zombie menace developed. . . and been caught in the open.

They put the horse in the associated stall with plenty of feed and water, and boarded it up so that zombies could not get in the openings. Zombies couldn't use tools any more than swords, so fairly simple precautions could balk them.

They made sure of the house, similarly, nailing boards across the windows, as zombies could break the glass with their unfeeling hands. Then they heated supper over the glass chimney of a kerosene lamp and settled in for the night, alternating watches.

Benny took the first shift again. Soon there were sounds. Zombies trying to get in!

Benny checked nervously, and verified it. Clumsy hands were reaching into windows, not caring that shards of broken glass were slicing them. Zombies didn't bleed anyway, or feel pain. But they couldn't get past the boards, and lacked the expertise or insight to remove them. Benny didn't wake the others, he just watched, clenching the haft of his sword, nervously making sure.

In due course Cycleze came to relieve him. "You didn't panic. That's good."

"I would have panicked if they had gotten inside."

"They'll all be here by morning," he said. "We'll be socked in."

"Are—are we doomed?"

"No. We want them to gather in close."

"We do?"

"Easier to wipe them out together."

"But suppose we—we get overwhelmed?"

"We won't be. There are things the Duke doesn't know, and you must not share what you learn here with him, or anyone else."

"I won't share," Benny promised. "But what doesn't he know?"

"Beranger is pretty much what he seems: a tough, experienced adventurer and warrior. I am not what I seem."

Benny hesitated. "I—am I allowed to ask?"

"You'll find out for yourself soon enough."

"You're not a human wizard?" Benny asked blankly.

"Yes and no...I am constrained to this human form most of the time, but it's not my true form, as I am not of this world. Likewise, while I'm experienced in the arcane arts of this realm, I have other powers I don't like to show. For example, I made you come with us."

"But that was just a spur of the moment thing. I just decided--" Benny broke off. "You put that thought in my mind? Telepathy?"

"Yes."

"But why? I'm hardly any use to you and Dale. You'd be better off without me."

"One danger when I lend my powers out is corruption. Dale likes the power I grant him, and uses it well, but he is slowly being corrupted by it. That will lead to mischief, in due course."

Benny thought about that. "And I'm not corrupted?"

"Not yet. It is my hope that as you become a man, you will remain on the straight course, and be a useful companion. I do need a companion, on occasion. One I can trust."

"I—I don't understand. I always try to do the right thing, but I have trouble knowing what the right thing is."

"Precisely. Continue questing for that right thing."

Benny was becoming increasingly confused. "I'll—I'll try. But I sure don't know how to handle a mob of hungry zombies."

"Go sleep. You'll see in the morning."

Benny obeyed, hoping the man wasn't crazy. What was he, if not human? And would this secret enable them to kill all the zombies? It was hard to make much sense of that. But if he really was crazy, why did Beranger put up with him? Ugly and mean as Beranger might be, he was not a man for foolishness.

But what was there to do, except sleep and hope for the best? And trust that all would become clear in good time.

In the morning they breakfasted, saw to the horse— there was a connecting door to the stable—and made ready for action.

"Now we need to get them all together," Cycleze said. "My power extends only so far, and after using it I will be severely weakened, so we will have only one chance. We have to hope that all or almost all the zombies have collected here, so that very few remain to be mopped up separately."

"We can get on the roof of the stall and attract their attention," Beranger suggested.

"But won't there be other zombies laying siege to other houses?" Benny asked. "All across the town? How can we get them all here?"

"No," Cycleze said. "There are no other sieges, because the living folk are dead and consumed. That is why they are orienting on us. If not stopped, they will then move on to other cities, like Galver Dorn."

"As the Duke surely knows," Benny said. "The townsmen wouldn't much like that."

"Then let's get on it," Beranger said briskly, hardly cracking a smile.

They made their way to the stall, where the horse was evidently nervous about the surrounding zombies, and they climbed a ladder to the roof. They stood there and gazed out across the landscape.

There were zombies as far as Benny could see, crowding thickly around the house. They were hungry, all right!

"Bring them in closer," Cycleze said.

Closer! They were already much too close for Benny's comfort.

Beranger stood on the edge of the roof and made a grandiose gesture. "Here, you morons!" he called. "Come and get it!"

"But if they can't see us or hear us, how will that get their attention?" Benny asked.

"Fresh zombies can see and hear a little," Beranger reminded him. "But mainly they just sense us as live meat. Maybe it's the heat of our bodies. Since normally live folk run from zombies, they can sense motion, and they close in on it. Do your part."

Benny stood at the other edge of the roof, and gestured and called similarly. He felt foolish, capering before such an audience, but saw that the zombies did respond, crowding closer. He was very glad they could not reach him.

Or could they? Now they were so densely packed that they formed a struggling mound as zombies clambered on top of zombies, not caring who got crushed below. Soon it was as high as the stall roof, and filling in closer. They would be on it before long. Benny held his sword nervously, ready to start slicing, but he knew that more would swarm over the cut up ones and overwhelm the few living folk.

"Any time, Cy," Beranger said. He was already slicing off limbs and heads as they projected over the roof. The smell was awful.

Benny glanced back at Cycleze, and saw the man manifest as a pillar to turquoise light. "Don't look!" Beranger warned, and Benny hastily averted his gaze as the light intensified.

It was like a silent explosion. The color seemed to reach out to bathe the zombies, and they melted into a single massive glob. In a few seconds the house was surrounded by a dark pool that flowed outward across the landscape and sank into the ground, leaving a glistening oily residue.

The zombies were gone.

The greenish-blue light faded. Benny knew it was now safe to look. Cycleze lay on the roof as if unconscious. He looked drained.

"Take it easy," Beranger said. "We'll go mop up the rest."

"Do so," Cycleze agreed, and closed his eyes as if sleeping.

"We can't just leave him!" Benny protested.

"He needs to be left alone. We're doing that."

Beranger led the way down the ladder into the stall, then into the house. "They won't be hard to find," he said. "They'll smell our living meat and come for us. Just hack them apart."

"What—what happened on the roof?" Benny asked, still amazed.

"He's an angel; a being of light from another dimension…what you saw was him assuming his true form. No creature can look directly at it without being stunned and maybe blinded, and for zombies, whose hold on life is less secure, it's worse. Any in the vicinity get dissolved, as you saw. But in this mortal realm Cycleze can't hold it long, and the effort depletes him. It will be several hours before he can get up and walk, and overnight before he is fully functional. That's when he needs a friend, so no one will go after him when he's vulnerable."

All Benny could think of was an incidental question. "Does—does Duke Dijon know about Cycleze?"

"No. He thinks we're just lucky. But he doesn't trust us, so he gives us the worst assignments. If we succeed, the dirty job is done. If we don't, he'll be rid of us. It's win-win."

"But I thought you and the Duke were friends!"

"Know this, lad: your worst enemies can be the friendliest to your face. Never trust anyone you don't really know."

"Then why do you go to him?"

"The money is good. It's also a challenge, sort of one-upmanship. Every time we complete a mission and live to tell the tale, we score points on him. He hates that."

"So we'll return to him for the second mission?"

"Which will be a worse stinker than this one," Beranger agreed, laughing.

Worse than this one. Benny repressed a shudder.

They walked on into the deserted town. Two zombies appeared from a house and charged them. Beranger neatly sliced one in half so that the pieces fell separately, while Benny nerved himself, held his breath, and managed to behead the other. The body still lumbered toward him, until he cut off a leg and it fell.

He had slain his first zombie.

"Congratulations," Beranger said. "You have been blooded. Or slimed, as the case may be."

Benny managed to hold his gorge.

They continued though the town, finding several more stray zombies.

They rounded a corner of a building. The door opened and a young woman emerged. She ran toward them, smiling, her brown hair flouncing.

Beranger lopped off her head with a backhand swing.

Blood gushed out as the woman fell.

She was alive.

Beranger faltered, staring at Benny with a look of guilt before resolution steeled his features. "She should've known better than to come charging at us like that…the heifer had it coming. But did you see the precision of that swing, Benny? Damn I'm good!"

Benny stared at Beranger and became uneasy. The man had taken an innocent life and made a joke of it. That as action bothered Benny far more then the mistake itself. Cycleze was right. Beranger was indeed being corrupted. He was too much into killing.

CHAPTER 9

They parked the wagon and stabled the horse at the edge of town, then walked on in. Cycleze evidently knew that their next mission would be close at hand.

"I am so glad to see you're safely back!" Duke Dijon exclaimed as they entered his office. He had of course known they were coming; they had made no secret of their arrival in Galver Dorn.

"And we are so glad to be back," Beranger said affably.

"Was it difficult?"

"It was a challenge, but we managed." And again, townsmen would already have verified that the zombies were gone. They would soon be recolonizing the freed real estate, as no original owners survived. "What's the other task?"

"Vampires."

"I don't like vampires," Beranger said.

"Nobody does. That's why it's a problem."

"That's why you saved this chore for us."

Dijon nodded. "We do seem to understand each other."

"Yes, we do," Beranger agreed. Both Cycleze and Benny kept straight faces; it was, after all, true. "Hand over the money and the info. We'll get it done."

The Duke produced another bag of gold, which Beranger verified while listening to the information.

"There was a wealthy recluse who lived in a mansion not far from town," Dijon said. "He had little contact with the locals, preferring to maintain his own personnel for servants and to grow his own grain and vegetables for his staff and stock. Thus the neighbors were not immediately aware when he died or departed—we remain uncertain which—as the mansion and grounds continued to be well-maintained. Occasionally a servant would be spied scything the lawn or clearing storm damage, so it seemed that all remained in order. Until one neighbor became suspicious. He set up a post in a tall tree just off the property and used a powerful spyglass to observe the mansion and its occupants. It took some time, but he was patient. He saw a man go to a cow in a back pen and bite the animal's neck, sucking its blood. They were vampires! They must have set up their coven when the owner left, and because they were secretive, the townsmen did not know." Dijon smiled grimly. "But now we do know, and naturally we want it promptly extirpated. We can't have vampires preying on us."

"They were feeding on the neighbors?" Beranger asked.

"No. They are canny enough to know that would be a dead giveaway of their nature. But they had to be preying on somebody. They can change to bats and fly to other sections, so as to keep the location of the coven private."

"But he was feeding on a cow," Benny protested.

"Obviously they maintain the stock as backup. Vampires prefer human blood."

"We'll get it done," Beranger said.

"Make sure you get them all. We don't want a re-infestation later."

"Tomorrow," Beranger agreed.

"Tomorrow will be fine."

Dijon gave them the address, and they left his office. "This doesn't sound too dangerous," Benny said. "Where's the catch?"

"You are thinking like a hunter," Beranger said approvingly. "We need to study the situation and find the catch before we strike. What do you think it is?"

This was another test. Benny focused. "They must be more deadly than we know. So when we come, they'll bite us and turn us into vampires."

"They won't do that."

Benny, guided by that, worked it out for himself. "Because they don't want more vampires. It's the predator prey ratio: the fewer the vamps, the more blood for each one of them. But they could still fight us and kill us."

"Not if we catch them by surprise."

Suddenly Benny saw it. "And we won't do that, because they'll know we're coming."

"And why will they know?"

"Because Dijon will tell them! Because he wants to be rid of us more than he wants to be rid of the vampires."

"Mixed," Beranger said.

"I read his mind," Cycleze said. "He wants to be rid of us both. So a fight to mutual destruction will suit him just fine."

"There must be more than that," Beranger said.

"There is. Vampires have infiltrated the political leadership of several other towns, and proved to be astute advisers. They are doing very well, and Dijon's illicit businesses are losing market share. So he wants to be rid of them, not because of any danger to the populace—he hardly

57

cares about the common folk—but as a business measure. He fears that this local coven is setting up to be a base to infiltrate his own shady personnel. So he wants them gone as an elementary precaution. Preferably in a way that does not implicate him, because they actually have human rights. He will of course deny sending us. If the vampires kill us, he can use that as a pretext to firebomb their mansion, thus being rid of both."

"I could get to dislike the Duke," Beranger muttered. "If I tried."

"So the catch is that it's a trap for us," Benny said. "How do we handle that?"

"We take them out," Beranger said. "In a way that implicates Dijon. So that the corrupt officials of the other towns come to regard him as a danger to them. That will be more than enough mischief for him, as they're as canny and unscrupulous as he is." He glanced at Cycleze. "You know where it is."

"Naturally. This way." They ducked into a house they were passing. This turned out to be a clothing depot, where the uniforms of the Duke's personal minions were stored. The odd thing was that the depot's personnel were all asleep.

Then Benny caught on: a sleep spell, well within Cycleze's power. And of course it had not been coincidence that they were in this vicinity; they had been headed for this depot all along.

Soon the three of them were outfitted in the Duke's distinctive blue livery. They walked out, and the people of the town pretended not to see them. It was dangerous to be openly curious about the Duke's business.

"Now what?" Benny asked Beranger.

"Now we take out the vamps."

"But that's tomorrow."

Beranger merely looked at him. Oh, he was being naive again. The Duke had been given the wrong day, so that their immediate action would catch him by surprise. He wouldn't even be able to protest their accomplishment of his mission early.

What impressed Benny the most was that Beranger had given that day when the Duke gave them the assignment. He had already planned this, then.

They marched on toward the address they had for the coven. Many people saw them, and would remember. Any of them could have told the Duke, but again, it was safest simply to mind their own business. Why question the Duke's activities?

"The vampires do not know we're coming at this time," Cycleze said. "There are thirteen of them, scattered around the premises."

"Kill any you encounter," Beranger told Benny. "Do not pause to talk with them any more than you would with a zombie. Just cut off their heads."

The estate was large. High palisades concealed it from its neighbors. They opened the front gate, which was not locked, and walked boldly up the drive to the mansion. They opened the front door, also not locked, and went in.

"Twelve on the ground floor," Cycleze said. "One upstairs."

They drew their swords. "Take that one," Beranger said to Benny. "We'll take out the others."

Benny didn't argue. The thought of killing anyone knotted his stomach, but he remembered the zombies. It had to be done. These dangerous creatures were a lot less human than they looked. He climbed the grand staircase in sight of the entrance.

Upstairs consisted of a hall with a number of doors, surely bedrooms. He gripped his sword tightly and opened the first, verifying its nature. It was empty. He opened the second, also empty.

When he opened the third he heard something. It sounded like water splashing. How could that be? Oh—it was a lavatory, in the corner of the bedroom. Someone was washing up!

He burst into the chamber, sword held high. And paused.

"Oh!" It was a girl, a young woman, nude, standing before a filled basin, with a sponge in her hand. She stared at him with dismay.

Benny knew what he should do: swing his sword to behead her. But two things stopped him. First, he remembered how Beranger had slain the living human woman, mistaking her for a zombie. Benny desperately did not want to make that mistake himself. Second, she was beautiful. She was sylphlike slender and well proportioned, with a lovely face and long fair hair extending past her pert bottom to her knees. Exactly the kind of damsel he'd despairingly longed for as a girlfriend.

"You're human," she said.

"Yes." He could think of no other response.

"I am a vampire. You can see my teeth." She bared her teeth, showing petite fangs.

Why hadn't she tried to hide her nature? "Yes."

"I think I know what you are here to do," she said. "You had better do it before you run out of time. I won't resist."

"I'm not here to rape you!" he protested.

"If you tie a towel around my head, I will not be able

to bite you. Then you can safely do it."

"No!" he cried in anguish.

"Then, what is your intention?"

"I—I--" But he could not say it.

"You are here to kill me. You can do that after you rape me."

He was emotionally overwhelmed. "May the gods curse me, I can't!"

"You will get in trouble with your friends if you don't. That is the nature of such encounters."

"How can you be so damned rational?"

"I have trained myself to be realistic and accept the inevitable. It isn't necessarily easy."

Benny was almost in tears. He was totally lost. He dropped his sword. "I can't hurt you. If you're going to bite me and escape, do it now."

Her eyes widened in surprise, an uncannily human expression. "You are sparing me?"

"Yes!"

She stepped toward him, graceful in her motion. "Then I must thank you."

Benny stood frozen as she came to stand directly before him, a vision of perfection. Her breasts lifted as she put her hands to his head and held it in place as her face approached. Her eyes were a pale red. He closed his own eyes tightly, bracing for the bite.

Then her mouth was up against his. She was kissing him! He felt as if he were flying.

She broke the kiss without retreating from his body. "Thank you," she said softly.

"You—you didn't bite me."

"You did not rape me or kill me."

His mind was whirling. "You spared me because I spared you?"

She smiled. "Also, you're cute."

"I—I--"

"Hold me, please. I am going to cry."

"Vampires can cry?"

"Oh, yes, when we have reason." Indeed, her eyes were brimming.

What could he do? He embraced her elegant form, and she cried against his shoulder, her tears soaking into the cloth.

After a time she drew back. "Thank you," she repeated. "It is not every day I am so severely threatened and reprieved. I am not emotionally equipped for it."

This was absolutely crazy. "I think I love you."

"Then I am yours."

She had not said she loved him back, and why should she? She was saying she would let him possess her, maybe in gratitude. "Uh, maybe you should get dressed. If you're through washing." He could hear the fighting downstairs, reminding him that the situation was urgent. The urges of a teenage boy in puberty had to wait.

"Yes. I had just finished gardening, and was dirty. I love working with earth, but I do need to clean up afterward. You surprised me." She stepped away from him and picked up bra and panties from the table behind her. She put them on, then added a simple red dress that matched her eye color. She donned matching socks and slipped her small feet into slippers. None of this detracted from her elegance. Finally she looked in the mirror and bound her hair back into a long ponytail.

"You can see yourself in the mirror?" he asked belatedly.

62

"Yes. I am completely human."

"But you're a vampire!"

"A human vampire," she agreed. "There are other types."

Despite the fear of his companions bursting in at any second, Benny's thoughts and gaze remained fixed on her. "I—I guess I don't know much about vampires."

"You are staring," she informed him gently.

"You're the most beautiful creature I've ever seen."

"Then I will forgive you the stare."

"I don't even know your name."

"I am Virtue."

"I am Benny."

"I am pleased to meet you, Benny," she said, catching his hand and formally shaking it.

"But—but vampires aren't virtuous." That had not come out at all the way intended. "I mean—I don't know what I mean."

"It is an aspiration. I aspire to be always virtuous. I don't always succeed."

"I'm sorry," he said, embarrassed. "I—I *really* don't know much about vampires."

"There was no need for you to know. We tend to be secretive."

"So—so how did you come to be named that?"

"I wish I could share all of my personal history with you, but there is little time for that now."

"Little time?" he asked somewhat blankly; the memories of Beranger and Cycleze had disappeared from his mind.

"I am sure you did not come here alone. Your friends will soon kill me, since you did not. But I will die satisfied that I had a boyfriend before my life ended."

"You're right! They'll kill you. Flee! Can you fly?"

"It takes time to transform to bat-form. At least half an hour. I do not believe I have that time." She gazed at him wistfully. "Besides, I do not want to leave you, now that I have found you, a genuinely compassionate young man." She glanced toward the bed. "Perhaps there is time to give you something to remember. I do not need to die a virgin."

The notion appealed phenomenally. Yet he argued. "But that would ruin your virtue!"

"Not when it is given in the spirit of mutual love. Virtue need not be so narrowly defined." She took his hand and led him toward the bed.

The door burst open. Beranger stood there, holding his sword, which was dripping red blood. "You didn't kill it!" he exclaimed. "I had hoped better for you."

"This is Virtue Vampire," Benny said. "I love her."

"She spelled you already!"

"She kissed me."

"That's what I said. She spelled you into captive love, to save her hide."

"No, she did not," Benny said.

"Sure she did!"

"She couldn't. I already loved her."

The baffled man paused briefly, mentally regrouping. "Well, we'll take care of that right now." Beranger advanced on Virtue, who faced him without flinching.

Benny jumped to stand between them. "You'll have to kill me first."

"You don't even have your sword! How can you fight?"

It was true. Benny's sword lay on the floor where he had dropped it. "I can't. I couldn't match you anyway. I'm just saying that you can't kill her until you kill me. I won't live without her."

Beranger stared at him. "You're serious!"

"Yes."

"You're crazy!"

"He's right," Virtue said. "I am doomed anyway, but you can live, Benny. I would rather have you live. Step aside."

"No."

"You're a fool," Beranger gritted. "But I'm not ready to kill you yet. Cycleze favors you, and I don't want to alienate him. So I will let you go, you and your vampire whore, this time."

A red cloud seemed to form over Benny's head. "Give me time to get my sword. Then say that again."

Beranger looked at him. Benny looked back, his rage fairly bursting out.

It was Beranger who backed down. "Get your sword and go," he said gruffly. "But if I ever see you again, I swear I will kill you."

"Please," Virtue said. "Do not fight."

That was a plea Benny could not deny. He fetched his sword and took her by the arm. They left the room, and the house.

At the edge of the estate they paused to gaze back at the mansion. Smoke was rising from it, and in moments flames licked out from the windows. They were burning it down!

"I'm sorry," Benny said. "About your coven. About your mansion. About this whole awful business."

"So am I," Virtue said. "But it seems it was destined. I will mourn my chosen family in my own time."

Now the townsmen were running toward the fire. "They'll see us!" Benny said, alarmed.

"I can help. I will make us easy to ignore."

"You can do that?"

"I have been learning magic. Nothing spectacular, but dull magic can be useful on occasion." She gripped his arm, and he felt a faint, odd pulse.

Then they walked on through the town to where the horse was stabled, hitched up the wagon, and departed, no one noticing them. They were on their way home.

Now Benny felt overwhelmed by the abrupt change in his life. He had lost his place in the trio and gained a lovely girlfriend…who was a vampire. What else could beat that?

Chapter 10

Despite the climactic end of Virtue's coven, the ride back to Gant was relatively peaceful. Since fetching the horse and wagon that his companions had abandoned, Benny had tried to keep Virtue's mind off recent events by telling her about his past. There wasn't much to tell, however, and after not too long Virtue felt compelled to share her story.

"I was a human child in an abusive family. I was beaten regularly for little cause, and it seemed that nothing I could do would benefit my status. I longed to escape, but I had nowhere to go. Then a vampire came to me one afternoon when I was playing in the dirt. She had come to feed on me, but desisted when she saw how young I was. She looked nice. 'Take me with you,' I begged her. 'I can't,' she said sadly. 'You're not a vampire.' 'Can't you bite me and make me one?' I asked. 'I could, but we take only those who really want to join us.' 'I really really want to,' I said. So she gave me the conversion bite. It didn't even hurt. The effect was not immediate, but I could feel it working inside me, slowly converting me to her kind. Then she took me by the hand and led me away. 'You must choose a name,' she told me. 'Virtue,' I said, because it was a word and a concept I liked, even as a child. So I joined her coven as Virtue, and had been happy there for the past ten years as I learned the ways of the vampires. But now that they're gone…" Virtue stopped at the memory of her family.

"I'm so sorry. I wish there was something I could do. I can't help but feel responsible somehow," Benny said.

"It's not your fault. You were only doing what you thought was right, but when you saw my true nature you showed mercy upon me. Were the members of my coven still alive, I'm certain they would not deem you guilty either."

"Still…" Virtue smiled kindly at Benny, placing her hand on his knee before glancing around at their method of transportation.

"Please, I do not wish to make mischief or change subjects," Virtue said, "but whose horse and wagon are these?"

"They belong to Laughing Jack Baldwin, the innkeeper. Now I am returning them." That was a simplification, but it would do.

"Will your friends be angry about losing this?"

"They're not my friends! The truth is, I'm glad to be rid of them. Especially now that they have slaughtered your coven."

"Still, it may be arguable who should have the wagon."

Benny shrugged. "It may be, but they'll know I have the right of the case. They can come and get it again from Jack if they have a mind."

She let it be, and they rode on. But it lingered in his mind. Was he wrong to take the wagon instead of walking? Beranger had said it was to be returned after this mission. Still, maybe not right now. Yet what about the two men intent on killing for money? What would be the ultimate fate of the horse in their hands? She had put his thoughts on a matter of ethics, and he wasn't sure he had made the correct decision.

Benny and Virtue got to know each other better as they traveled. She filled him in on the culture of the vampires, who it seemed did not necessarily prey on humans. Her own coven had not, preferring the animals, which they treated well. Also, they did not feed entirely on blood; it was merely a portion of their diet, as meat was for humans. It provided them with what they needed to perform magic. So the case against the vampires was seriously flawed.

Something else bothered him. Beranger had taught him to question things, to look gift horses in the mouth. Sometimes it made a significant difference. Now he addressed Virtue. "I hate doing this, but I have to question you more closely."

"Yes, it was not coincidence that you spied me naked."

He looked at her, startled. "You knew I would ask!"

"You are ignorant, not stupid, and you need to know the truth."

"You amaze me! I—I hope it is not a bad truth."

"It is a terrible truth, but no fault of yours or mine. We all do what we must do, though sometimes we do not like it."

Benny focused on the trail ahead as they rode north through the forest. "About doing what we must. We—we understood that we had to kill the vampires, but that there might be political connections. That they might be warned, so that we would get wiped out tomorrow as they sprang their trap. So we struck today, by surprise. I—I thought any vampire I encountered would come flying at me with bared fangs and I would have to kill it to defend myself. To stop an ugly monster. Instead there was you: so lovely, so innocent. I can't kill you, Virtue, no matter what the truth is. I know I'm just a foolish boy, but I do think I love you. I know you don't love me; how could you? So I think I am ready to hear your truth."

"We saw the three of you enter the compound," she said. "Our head man did a quick skry and learned that we were doomed."

"A what?"

"A skry. He gazed in a crystal and saw the near future."

"Oh. Magic."

"Yes, of course. We are magical creatures, as I said."

"Couldn't you have fought? You outnumbered us."

"No. We are pacifist."

So the men had cut down unresisting vampires, male and female. No glory there, and no honor. "Damn."

"There was only one way any of us could escape," she continued. "That was me, the youngest and, well, most appealing. I could survive only if I won the heart of the youngest invader and stayed with him. That was you. I did that by arranging to show you my bare body so that your youthful impulse would be to use me sexually. Young men tend to get emotional about their sexual partners. I knew I had to submit or die, and I didn't want to die. So I encouraged you to take me, trusting that then you would want to keep me alive."

"Yes! Only--"

"Only you didn't take me, so it was incomplete and my survival remained uncertain. I kept trying. Then your man with the awful face came, and I knew if you opposed him you would put your own life at risk. There was no point in that. So I knew the ploy had failed. You were such a nice boy I didn't want you to die, too. Then--"

"Virtue, I don't want to use you sexually! I mean, I guess I do, but not that way. I want to marry you!"

She shook her head. "You can't mean that. You hardly know me."

"And of course you don't want to marry me. I understand that. I'm just a foolish kid."

"How old are you, Benny?"

He was surprised by the question. "I'll be seventeen next month. Why?"

"I will be seventeen next week. We are close in age."

"But not in nature. You're absolutely beautiful, while I'm nothing."

"You are everything. Benny, I do want to marry you, but that is because the skry indicated that my survival is linked to you. I can give you sex freely, but it would not be fair to marry you without loving you. So--"

She would marry him? "Can't we just shut up and kiss?"

She laughed. "This is foolish."

"I know," he said disconsolately.

"Foolish," she repeated. "But I'm young and foolish too." Then she caught his head as she had before, turned it to face her, and kissed him so passionately he thought he might pass out.

She gave him a minute to recover, while the horse plodded on. Then she spoke again. "Sex comes and goes, but marriage is forever. Suppose we make this compromise: wait until we are both 18, then if you still want to marry me, you can do so. But there are constraints. For the most sincere marriage, we must not share sex beforehand, only after we are wed. So that I remain pure for the occasion. That may be a hard route for you. So if you prefer to have me as a mistress instead, we can do that now."

He hated being so wickedly tempted. "What—what would you prefer?"

"I prefer marriage; it is far more binding. But the choice is really yours, not mine. You are the man. The human."

"Marriage!" he said. "And maybe you'll love me by then."

"That is quite possible. You evince sterling qualities, especially of conscience."

"I just want to be with you."

"And I with you, albeit perhaps for different reasons. Then shall we consider ourselves affianced?"

"Yes!"

"Yes," she echoed.

They came to the fork where the giant's trail joined the main route. Benny guided the horse to the lesser one. Virtue looked askance.

"There's a place to stop safely for the night," he explained.

"I could change to bat form and hide in a tree."

"Oh, Virtue, I'd rather sleep with you in my arms."

"You may do that," she agreed.

"But what do *you* want?"

"I want what you want. But if you hold me in darkness, you may do something that will compromise my purity for our marriage."

"I—I—will risk that. We can keep our clothes on."

"As you wish."

"But bat form—all vampires can do that?"

"Yes. It is part of our magic. It enables us to travel without attracting attention."

"Then why didn't you all become bats and fly away from the mansion?"

"We did not have time. Your element of surprise was effective."

"Oh, Virtue, I'm so sorry!"

"So am I. But we don't always have convenient choices."

They came to the stronghold. "Do—do you eat any regular food? Like pancakes?"

"Yes. It is merely that blood is a necessary part of our diet, as meat is part of yours. I will eat your pancakes."

He laughed. "You're just like a regular girl!"

"I *am* a regular girl. With some magic."

He was more than ready to settle for that.

They slept in the loft, clothed, embraced, kissing every so often. He felt as if he was in a subsection of heaven. They did not compromise her purity.

Next day they reached the Fox Den Inn. Laughing Jack came out to meet them. "You brought back the horse and wagon! You found a girl! A lovely one."

"This is Virtue, my fiancée. She's a vampire."

Jack rocked back. "Joke?"

"No joke, Mr. Baldwin," Virtue said, briefly baring her fangs. "Benny saved my life, and I will marry him. I mean no harm to you or yours."

"There must be a considerable story there," Jack said. "I will want to hear the whole of it, in due course. You'll share Benny's bed?"

"No," Benny and Virtue said almost together. Then Benny explained. "I want her to be pure for marriage when we're 18."

"I don't have another nook for a person to sleep. Just yours and Nadia's."

"I can turn bat and hang from a rafter."

"The cook would freak out. She'd be sure you'd drop

guano in the turnip soup."

"Maybe Virtue can share with Nadia," Benny suggested.

"You know, I had a dream last night," Jack said. "That Nadia would have to do something she didn't want to do, but that it would pay her well to do it. Maybe that's it."

Soon they braced Nadia. "You want me to share with a vampire?" Nadia asked, appalled. "Mosquitoes are bad enough blood suckers; I don't need a big one."

"She won't suck your blood," Benny said.

"So you say. If you're so trusting, *you* sleep with her."

"I think I can settle this," Jack said. "We can use the Oath of Sober Jack."

The others looked at him.

"Sober Jack was my father. He renovated the Fox Den and moved here from Alsbury. Sometimes he had trouble with customers, so he worked out a way to make them behave. He devised the Oath."

"Is that what you made that drunk wagoner swear months ago?" Nadia asked. "I thought it was a joke."

"That wagoner behaved, didn't he? The Oath is self-enforcing as long as the one who swears it is on the premises, which is really all I care about. So Virtue can swear not to suck Nadia's blood, and she won't have to worry."

"You're a great guy, and a good employer, and I love you, Jack," Nadia said. "But sometimes you're so full of crap it's a wonder you don't explode before you get to the outhouse."

"I'll prove it," Jack said. "Benny, Virtue, Nadia: swear by Sober Jack not to drink any cider for the next hour. Then try to do it."

"I love your cider," Benny said.

"So do I," Nadia said. "'Specially when it's just turning

hard. I have to watch that I don't get tipsy and let a customer feel me up."

"Make the oath. We all know it's not serious. This is just a demonstration."

The three were similarly perplexed, but made the oath. Then Jack brought out brimming mugs of cider for each of them. "Drink up!"

Benny stared at his mug. He was unable to bring it to his face. He saw Virtue and Nadia similarly incapacitated.

"What's keeping you?" Jack demanded. "Do you want to waste it on a wagoner?"

They all tried, and tried again. They simply couldn't do it.

"Have I made my point?" Jack asked. "If you want to drink that cider, you'll have to wait an hour, or take it outside, beyond the range of dearly beloved Sober Jack."

Benny looked longingly at his mug. "Maybe we'd better do that, rather than let it go to waste."

The three of them went outside, trying repeatedly to drink. Only when they got well away from the inn were they able to do it.

"I will make that oath," Virtue said when they returned to the inn. "I swear by Sober Jack to suck no person's blood and do no one here any harm, ever."

"That will do," Jack said.

"I will share my bed," Nadia said. "Though I can't see how it will pay me to do so." She shrugged. "But Jack's had visions before, and they've always come true."

Thus it was settled. Virtue moved in with Nadia, and the two soon were great friends. Nadia gave her pointers on handling drinking customers. "You have to learn not to jump and spill the ale when one grabs your ass."

"When one does what?"

"They're *men*," Nadia said dismissively. "They grab. They're not supposed to, but any time Jack's not watching, they do. They think it's funny when you scream and drop a mug. You've got the world's cutest ass; they'll be on you like, well, like men."

"I couldn't handle that. I am promised to Benny, and he does not do that."

Benny was silent. He would have loved to grab an ass, but hadn't had the courage, and now of course he would not.

They went to Jack, explaining the problem. "I'll take care of it," he promised.

Next day when the men gathered, Jack took the floor. "We have a new bar girl and waitress," he said, indicating Virtue, who was now in a Fox Den skirt, looking as pretty as only she could be. "She's a vampire."

The men stared, startled.

"Show 'em your fangs, honey," Jack said.

Virtue briefly bared her fangs.

"She has promised not to bite anyone here," Jack continued. "Not unless someone really wants her to."

There was laughter. Naturally nobody wanted to be bitten by a vampire, even such a pretty one.

"The way you will signal your desire to be bitten is by grabbing her butt."

There was a sudden chill.

"Go serve that man a mug, honey," Jack told Virtue, indicating a customer who was in on the demonstration.

She carried a brimming mug of ale to the man. He slowly reached toward her midsection. She twitched her lip, exposing one fang. His hand quickly changed course and went to the mug. The others laughed. The point had been made.

But though Virtue was popular as a waitress, and she did her share of other chores such as washing the pots, her favorite job was gardening. The garden in back soon flourished, producing splendid turnips. Turnip soup became more popular than ever. Benny suspected that it was not simply that the turnips were excellent, but that the men liked eating what they knew Virtue had handled, in that manner getting a small piece of her.

Jack brought in an old book of magic. "This covers many things, including a section on vampires," he said. "It can never replace your lost coven, Virtue, but it may have some useful information."

"Our head vamp had a similar tome," she said. "Oh, thank you, Jack!" She kissed him on the cheek. It was plain that they liked each other in much the way Jack and Benny liked each other, like parent and child.

Virtue delved into the book once the day's chores were done. "Oh, this is wonderful!" she said. "It tells me how to fill out my powers. Only--"

"Only you need practice," Nadia said.

"Yes. It has a whole chapter on bites, ranging from sedative to healing to potency. But to make them work properly I need to zero them in, and I can't do that without actually trying them to see how they work. I wouldn't do it, even if I were not bound by Sober Jack's Oath."

"You swore to suck no blood and do no person here harm," Jack said.

"Yes. I feed on no person."

"I happen to have a date tonight with a lady I know. I would like to impress her in bed, and believe she is amenable, but fear that if I try I will fall short and embarrass myself.

I'm simply not young any more. Did you mention potency?"

"Yes. There is a bite that--" She broke off, looking at him. "You want that bite!"

"Let's say that I offer myself as a test subject. I do not believe that such a bite would harm me, so it wouldn't violate the Oath, and I would be gratified if I could gratify the lady."

Virtue looked at Benny and Nadia. "Could I really do that without violating the Oath?"

"Try it and see," Nadia said. "If it's harmful, the Oath won't let you do it."

Virtue nodded. She quickly reread that portion of the book, then approached Jack. "Give me your arm."

He presented his arm. She bent to put her fangs to his forearm, biting him lightly. "That should have some effect in a while," she said. "If I have done it correctly."

"I will let you know," Jack said, rising perhaps in more than one sense. He quickly departed.

"Is he just trying to encourage me?" Virtue asked.

"I don't think so," Nadia said with a smirk. "I've seen that reaction before. I think he felt the rush coming on and had to get with the woman in a hurry."

"Oh." Virtue blushed. She had evidently focused on the technical nature of the bite, rather than its practical effect.

Next morning Jack gave his report. "I did her four times before dawn. Next time mute it a bit, okay?"

Virtue laughed, relieved, though she blushed again. "I thought it wouldn't be enough."

"It was more than enough."

"They told me at the coven that I had enormous potential. I didn't believe them."

"Believe them," Jack said. He smirked. "Enormous is certainly the word." That caused another blush.

"Can you do sedative on me?" Nadia asked. "It's that time of the month, and I know I'll have trouble sleeping because of the cramps."

"I will try," Virtue said, and bit her lightly on the arm.

It worked. Nadia slept soundly through the night, and was in no discomfort when she woke.

There was an obnoxious customer. "This guy is mischief," Jack murmured to Benny. "Now I'm sorry I don't have Liverwart here."

Benny had an idea. "Could you give me strength?" he asked Virtue.

"Yes." She bit him on the arm. It was almost like a kiss. Immediately he felt the power surging through his body.

Meanwhile the situation was coming to a head. "I'll have to ask you to leave," Jack told the man.

"Yeah? Make me, old timer."

Benny walked up. "This way, sir," he said politely, indicating the door.

The man looked at him and laughed. "Get out of my face, kid, before I feed you your own foot."

"This way," Benny repeated, taking the man by the arm and squeezing.

The man stared, not so much in pain as in surprise. It was a very strong grip. Then he tried to jerk his arm away.

It didn't come. Instead Benny held on, used his other hand to catch that man's belt behind him, braced himself, and heaved. The man came off the floor, then landed on his face.

"Why you little--" he started.

Benny caught him by the collar as he rose, and hauled him across the room to the door. The man was helpless to resist that force. Benny threw him out the doorway.

The other customers were staring. Benny didn't know what to say.

Jack came to his rescue. "Thank you, Benny," he said, as if it were routine. "I'm sorry you had to do that. I trust we'll have no more rogues like him." He had clearly caught on to the bite, having had his own experience.

That was all, but thereafter Benny was treated with more respect. There were no more difficult customers. He did feel tired as the bite wore off; his added strength had been drawn from his bodily reserves. So it was not something to do casually.

Virtue also practiced changing into her bat form, so she could quietly fly off to feed on a forest animal. She got so she could do it in under ten minutes, which was very fast for a vampire.

Jack found an old crystal ball. "Maybe you can practice skrying," he suggested.

"Yes!"

Virtue practiced with the ball, learning to skry. She got to see a few hours into the future, then a day, but it was difficult. "There are so many paths," she said. "So many things that can happen that it becomes fuzzy. I need to be very specific, or it's hopelessly vague."

"Try one on me," Benny suggested.

She did. And smiled. "Tonight you will kiss me."

"Uh, yes, of course. But is there anything out of the ordinary?"

She stared into the crystal. "Not tomorrow. Not next week. But there is something in your future. Danger. Fighting. Pain. Maybe death." She wrenched her gaze away. "Oh, Benny, whatever you plan, don't do it! It's dangerous!"

"But I don't plan anything except being with you."

"That I fear is part of the danger. Not from me, but because of me."

"Maybe some other man wants you, and wants to fight me for you."

"Maybe," she agree uncertainly. "I'm not a possession. But if someone thought I was, there might be trouble."

From him, Benny thought. "I think I'd better practice my fighting."

"I dislike this, for I don't like fighting. Remember, I'm a pacifist. But after what happened to my coven, I am not sure that pacifism is right in all cases."

"I'll practice," Benny said.

Thereafter he did, working with knife, sword, and club, building up his body and his skills.

But perhaps the greatest success was the dance. A customer remarked that a tavern in a far town had a dancing act with pretty girls. So, for a joke, they tried it, adapting dance moves for a trio. Then, costumed, Benny performed it with the two girls. Both were fair-haired, and their unbound tresses flung out as they moved, enhancing the effect. He made grand gestures while the girls whirled in their skirts, showing their legs. Nadia was buxom, with solid thighs, and made a very good impression on the men. In fact, she was sexy as hell. But Virtue, slender throughout, had an ethereal quality of loveliness that transformed the scene.

The applause was considerable. They decided to do it regularly.

And day-by-day, the tavern business increased. Men came, certainly, but so did women, and they all raptly watched the dance.

"Don't you get jealous?" Benny overheard a woman ask Nadia. She didn't need to say of whom.

81

"No. She's my friend, and she helps me, and she's good for business." All true.

What no one said was that the coven's judgment was being more than vindicated. Virtue had truly great potential, now being translated into performance.

Benny was with her daily, as thoroughly in love as ever. And Virtue was open about her gradually increasing feeling for him. She expected to love him completely by the time they were married. They passed their seventeenth birthdays and headed toward the eighteenth.

The idyll seemed almost too good to last.

CHAPTER 11

Bad news came suddenly. The giant Liverwart had been in and out, doing chores as needed, but less had been needed since Virtue came, in significant part because customers behaved better in her presence. Even the job of occasional bouncer had been preempted by Benny, thanks to the vampire's strength bite. "Need help!" he cried.

Laughing Jack gave him his immediate attention. It turned out that his entire clan had been slain by men resembling Beranger and Cycleze.

Jack was grim. "This must be what you've been practicing for, Benny. Those two, whoever they are, have to be stopped."

"Beranger said he'd kill me if he ever saw me again," Benny said.

"We don't know it's him. I know him; he's a good man at heart. He wouldn't do something like this for no reason. Maybe somebody's trying to frame him, to get him into trouble."

"That must be," Nadia said. "Dale's not like that."

Benny was not all sure they were correct, but he didn't care to argue the case. The one regarded the man as a friend;

the other as a love object. "I will go."

"There is danger," Virtue protested. "Remember my skry."

"That's why I have been practicing." But if it really was Beranger, Benny knew he was no match for the man. He had put on weight and strength, and learned some skill with his weapons, but the other was a master. Benny was determined not to delude himself; therein lay death.

"Not danger directly to you. Not immediately. But you will learn horrible things, and it will change you. Now I am coming to understand my obscure skrying." She gazed at him tearfully. "You may not return to me."

"Honey, you will always have a place here regardless," Jack said, and Nadia nodded. They both liked her, and so did the customers.

"I never want to leave you!" Benny said. "But I have to help Liverwart if I can." As he spoke, he realized that there was a tinge of guilt for his part in the slaying of the other giant, Kidneywart. He did have to do what he could.

"Then I must come with you," Virtue said. "To share your fate."

"But there might be violence."

"Yes. I can't be violent myself, but maybe I can help shield you from violence and make your way easier."

Benny realized that he would much rather have her with him, but he didn't want to make such a selfish decision himself. "Jack, Nadia—what do you say?"

Nadia had an idea. "Jack, your vision said Virtue would really help me, some day. Does this relate?"

"I don't know. Maybe Virtue could skry that."

Skry a former vision? Benny was dubious.

"I will try," Virtue said. She fetched the crystal ball and

stared deeply into it. "Yes, it relates. I don't know how; there is much danger, much obscurity, and I fear much ugliness, but that much is clear."

"Maybe you can clear Dale." And there was Nadia's personal interest, as she still carried the torch for the man.

"Maybe," Virtue agreed. Benny knew she was as doubtful about Beranger as he was. Neither Jack nor Nadia had seen how ugly the man could be.

"Then you must go, my dear friend Virtue," Nadia said. "Though we will really miss you."

Jack spread his hands. "How can I argue? But I beg you, kids, be careful. We need you for the dance." It was a whole lot more than that, but none of them wanted to address the complicated factors. Suppose it *was* Beranger?

They decided to walk, because it wasn't far. Virtue undressed, handed Benny her clothing, slowly assumed bat form and flew up to perch on Benny's shoulder. The giant looked startled; he had not seen this transformation before, and maybe not a naked girl either. Then Liverwart picked him up and set him on *his* shoulder. They were on their way.

Benny looked back as they sped along the trail. Jack was holding Nadia, and they both looked as if they were crying. Yes, they cared, and they feared much more than they said.

"Was it Beranger?" Benny asked the dread question as he rode high up.

The giant was unsubtle. "Yes."

Damn, on more than one score. "You know, Beranger killed a giant before," Benny said. "Kidneywart."

"He bad giant," Liverwart said.

"Maybe Beranger got the idea that all giants were bad." He was trying to be fair to the man.

And all Vampires?

That was Virtue's thought; he recognized her tone of mind, and of course she was perched right beside his head. She was working on another talent: telepathy!

"Know better. Kill anyway."

There it was. Jack might stand by the man, but Beranger had gone bad. Did that mean that Benny would have to fight him? There were several problems with that: Beranger had been his friend, of a sort, teaching him valuable things; Nadia wanted to marry the man; and Benny doubted he could defeat him in fair combat.

Damn, damn, damn.

Virtue, perched on his shoulder, sent another thought. *I feared this.*

Precisely. It was reasonably easy to do right when right and wrong were clear, but real life so often presented unkind compromises. Benny hardly knew what he was supposed to do. But as Jack would say, what would be, would be.

They arrived at the fringe of the giants' camp, and Liverwart set Benny down on the ground. Then Virtue flew down and resumed her human form. Benny handed her her clothes.

"Wow," the giant said, having gotten another good eyeful as she slowly transformed. Benny wasn't sure whether that was for her transformation from a tiny flying creature to a human woman, or for the eye-popping proportions of that woman.

Virtue smiled at Liverwart. "Thank you."

So it was proportions.

Now they entered the camp. It was an immediate horror. All the giants were dead: male, female, children, lying where they had been slain, their blood soaking into the ground. Their huge bodies had not yet cooled completely.

Liverwart did not know what to do; that was why he had come to the inn, where smarter friends were to be found. Now it fell to Benny to be his guide.

"First we must check the area to see if any survive, only seeming dead," he said. "We must locate the men who did this and deal with them. Then we must bury your friends, and you will have to move closer to the inn where at least you will have some company."

"Um," the giant agreed, relieved to have direction.

They scouted the area, but no giants survived. Then they discovered something remarkable: Cycleze, lying under a tree, stabbed multiple times, plainly dying. His skin was peeling away to reveal bright turquoise light beneath. It had never occurred to Benny that the mancould die; he was after all an angel.

First things first. "Where's Beranger?" Because that was the one he had to fight.

"He is gone. We fought, and I injured him; he must be alone to heal."

So there was no immediate danger from that quarter. Benny was only partly relieved. There was obviously a lot more to learn.

"Liverwart, the man who did this is gone," Benny said. That was a simplification, necessary for this person. "Bury the bodies while I try to find out more about why this happened."

"Um," the giant agreed, glad to have something to occupy him.

Benny turned to Virtue. "This is one of the men who killed your coven members. He is dying. I must talk to him and learn what I can before he dies. You don't have to stay."

"I will ease his pain," she said, kneeling beside Cycleze.

87

"I am your enemy, vampire," Cycleze said. "You have no call to help me."

She put her hand on his forehead. "I must help who I can. I can't mend you, but I can comfort you."

The man relaxed as the pain eased. "You are an angel."

"No, you are the angel."

"I am a fallen angel. You are an angel of mercy. That is better."

Benny agreed emphatically. But there were things he needed to know, and not much time to learn them. "Why did you kill the giants? They were no threat to you."

"True," Cycleze said. "This was Dale's mischief. He has a killing lust that increases daily. I thought I could control him, but he was going out of control, and finally he turned against me." He smiled weakly. "I would have been better off with you, Benny."

"Why did you want to be with anyone? You're not really human."

"I am fallen. I am doomed to reside among the mortals. So I resolved to make my stay on Earth as comfortable as possible, by amassing a fortune and using it to support a life of ease. To purchase ideal property, hire stout manservants to perform all necessary maintenance chores, and engage lasciviously lovely maidservants to cater to my personal inclinations. But I needed a man I could trust to guard my back, one not corrupted by greed or lust. A man like you, Benny, once you mature. Money makes many things feasible." He glanced at Virtue. "I could never have hired you, my dear."

"Never," she agreed without rancor.

Because she was not moved by any desire for riches or power, only by what was necessary and what was right.

She was not for sale.

"Benny is blessed to have you with him."

"Thank you."

Cycleze returned his attention to Benny. "With you beside me, as I said, I could have safely used those riches, because you are moral at heart. That is part of what Virtue sees in you, in case you were wondering."

Virtue did not deny it.

"But Dale caught on that you were being honed as a possible replacement for him. That is why he banished you, and I could not prevent it."

"He said it was because I interceded to save a vampire," Benny protested.

"An attractive vampire he would gladly have raped and degraded. But to get at her, he would have had to kill you, and then I would have killed him. He couldn't risk that at the time, so he banished you both, hoping at some later date to have a pretext to kill you and take her then."

"I would not have gone with him!" Virtue protested.

"You would not have had a choice, my dear. He would have bashed out your fangs and held you down for the occasion, and killed you when he finally tired of you. He has no respect for your virtue."

She was silent, knowing it was true.

"Benny, there is history you need to know before you encounter Dale again. He is a man of strong passions. Good and evil war constantly in him, and slowly evil is winning. Could that but be stifled, then he might be able to apply himself to positive endeavors. But I think that case has become hopeless."

"Yet he was good to me," Benny said somewhat reluctantly.

"He was grooming you similarly: to be his trusted companion and friend after I was gone." Cycleze smiled weakly. "It was not a woman that came between us, for we have different tastes; it was you."

"You—the two of you—I thought you were friends."

"We were two people with a common purpose. That is not the same. It requires a certain innocence to be a true friend. We were not innocent."

"I—I guess there was a lot I did not understand."

"And your lack of understanding becomes you."

Benny wasn't sure whether that was really a compliment. He was also dismayed to see Virtue's slight nod of agreement. "What is the history you wish to tell me?"

"You remember how the orcs massacred those children at the orphanage, long ago? How Dale's brother had been killed by an orc? How he organized a party to get revenge on those orcs? How he took on a dozen orcs single-handedly and got his terrible scar from that encounter?"

"Yes, Jack told me that history."

"That is false history."

Both Benny and Virtue stared at him. "False?" Benny asked.

"It was Beranger who killed the children at the orphanage in Alsbury."

Benny was appalled. He didn't want to believe it, but he knew that dying people seldom lied, and Virtue's glance signaled that Cycleze was telling the truth. "But why?"

"In order to make the townsmen hunt down the orcs he believed killed his brother."

"He believed?"

"Those orcs were peaceful. His brother's death had been an accident."

"You're sure?"

"Yes. I helped Dale mutilate the bodies of the orphans and place them into strange sexual positions." Cycleze smiled grimly. "Nothing sets off folk like sexual abuse. Minds click off and passion rules."

"But—but why not simply tell Dale the truth? That the orcs were blameless?"

"That was my crime. I manipulated Dale's mind into thinking that the orcs were responsible for his brother, meaning to cement our relationship. I didn't know he was going to kill the children, but by then it was too late to backtrack. I grieve for those innocents, the orcs and the children, and curse my part in that horror."

"All—all because you wanted to make Dale a friend, to support you as you amassed wealth?"

"Originally, yes. I was uncertain of my place in this realm, and wanted the reassurance of a knowledgeable native. Like a person starting a rock rolling down a steep hill, not realizing that it will start an avalanche that kills many others."

Benny's mind was whirling. "You—where did you come from?"

"It is hard to convey the concept, because you have no experience with anything beyond your own concept of reality. I am an inter-dimensional being who was expelled from my own dimension when I inadvertently annoyed a higher deity. Fallen angel is the closest concept your mythology presents. That's what Dale always called me at least."

Benny sighed, holding on to what he could understand. "The orcs were innocent."

"The orcs came and tried to stop Dale from mutilating

the children's bodies, knowing that they would get the blame. That's when he fought them. That is actually how he received the scar and lost his nose. The fight was real, but there was no glory in it."

Benny began to apply what he had learned from being with Beranger and Cycleze before. This story, horrible and true as it might be, was incomplete. "Why are you telling me this now? Wouldn't it be easier just to leave me to my ignorance, instead of knowing how bad you and Dale really were?"

"Easier, yes. Satisfactory, no. I want to confess my evils before I pass from this realm. And to do what little I can to ameliorate them. Maybe by doing so I'll be allowed to return home once this vessel is dead."

"What could you possibly do now?"

"Tell you the rest of the truth. Then tell you how you can defeat Dale in fair combat, so as to rid the world of him. Give you money and greatly extend your life. So that you can be a benefit to this world, instead of a liability as Dale and I were."

Benny stared at him. "I'm a 17-year-old stripling with a vampire girlfriend. How can you place any such trust in me?"

"I was wrong to recruit Dale. I am wiser now, and I think not wrong to recruit you. Wealth, power, and life in your hands will be forces for good rather than evil."

"This is ridiculous! I have earned no such trust."

Cycleze glanced at Virtue, who still had her hand on his forehead, abating his pain and perhaps reading his mind. "You know this young man well. Am I mistaken, vampire?"

"I think not," Virtue said.

"Benny, you must do two things to have a hope of defeating Dale, for he is more than your match as a warrior."

He smiled wincingly. "More than mine, as it turned out. I was going to kill him in his sleep after we finished with the giants, and take the money. I'm no saint either. But he caught on, and attacked me, and I will die. You must be better prepared than I."

"Two things?" Benny asked blankly.

"First, cut your hair."

Benny thought he had misheard. "Do what?"

"Virtue can skry to verify it. I do not know why, but it is necessary."

Was the man verging into nonsense as his body died? "What else?"

"Have Virtue give you the berserker bite."

"The what?"

"She will explain. I am fading and must cover the rest quickly." He winced as he reached into his jacket. "Here is a map. It shows where Dale keeps all of his gold that is not on his person. That gold will be yours after you kill him."

"I don't want to kill him!"

"You may not have a choice, any more than Virtue would if he got hold of her. You will kill him, or he will kill you."

That seemed all too likely to be true. And of course he had to try to stop the man from getting Virtue; the thought of her being brutally violated bothered him more than his own possible death.

"And here is the last of it," Cycleze said. "Give me your hand."

Benny glanced again at Virtue. She nodded. He took the man's cooling hand.

"I bequeath to you my remaining power in this dimension, which should prolong your life for several centuries, if you don't get killed first."

"Several centuries!"

Then a surge of life force passed from the fallen angel's hand to Benny's hand, and on into his body, invigorating it, and he knew it was true. He could live for centuries, if he didn't get killed.

Cycleze's hand dropped away. Virtue removed her hand from his forehead. "He is going," she said.

"Going?" Because it seemed he was already dead.

The man's body began to glow, as it had when he melted the zombies. Benny turned his eyes away to protect them, and so did Virtue.

A turquoise glow formed, illuminating the surrounding landscape. It faded.

When they looked again, all that remained was the man's clothing, limp on the ground. He had transformed back to the angel and departed from this dimension.

"I think he was not a bad angel, taken as a whole," Virtue said by way of benediction.

Benny could only agree.

CHAPTER 12

There was one more detail: the clothing. "Do we bury it, in lieu of his body?" Benny asked. "I don't think anyone else here can use it." It was too big for him, too small for the giant, and completely wrong for Virtue.

"That may be best," Virtue agreed. "Only--"

He looked at her quizzically. "There is a caution?"

"His special pipe."

Now Benny saw it lying there, with its twin bowls. The man had put tobacco in one, and some other substance in the other to get a mix of smokes. "I don't know. It shouldn't be wasted."

"You might take up smoking," she said teasingly.

"Why would I ever do that!"

She stooped to pick up the pipe. "There is magic. I can feel it. Maybe you *should* smoke it."

Benny shrugged. "I'd just cough and turn green." That was what had happened the one time he tried to smoke before, and the experience had discouraged him from ever trying again. But now he wondered.

There was a small pouch amidst the clothing. This turned out to have two compartments. One contained tobacco, the other something like aromatic sawdust.

"There's magic," Virtue repeated. "Not harmful."

"All right, stop nagging me. I'll try it."

She smiled. She never nagged him; anything she wanted, he wanted. If she felt magic in the pipe and pouch, he wanted to know its nature. A little bit of magic could go a long way.

He took the pipe, put some tobacco in one bowl and some of the fragrant sawdust in the other. Then he struck a light and sucked on the stem, fully expecting to draw in choking vapor and gag or try to cough his lungs out.

Instead it was something else. Vapor, yes, but not choking. It was more like breathing a rich confection of flower garden aroma. For an instant he felt dizzy; then his mind clarified.

"What is it, dear?" she asked.

Had she just called him dear? "I—suddenly I have a new—a rare new perspective. The world seems not to be different, but I can see it from another angle. I can make judgments I never could before."

"It must be mind clarifying," she said. "That can be useful."

"It can indeed," he agreed. "I will keep this."

Virtue carefully folded the clothing and tucked it into a crevice in the nearest tree. "This will mark the spot," she said. "For whatever that is worth."

"Yes." He emptied the spent ash and put away the pipe. Somehow he knew already that he would never be without it.

They helped Liverwart complete the burial of the bodies. The giant looked miserable, understandably; all his clan had been killed, and this was somehow making it final.

"I can help you somewhat," Virtue told Liverwart. "If you accept it, I will give you an emotional healing bite. It won't bring back your clan companions, but it will make you hurt less for losing them."

The giant looked uncertainly at Benny. "Do?"

Benny had to make an ethical choice. What was best for a simple-minded person? To stifle his grief, or allow it full expression? Given that the problem could not be fixed, an adjustment of attitude was probably best. "Do," he agreed.

Liverwart sat down on the ground, and Virtue bit him gently on the shoulder. For a moment there seemed to be no change. Then the giant smiled. "Hurt less."

Benny had another idea. "Maybe you should go take over Kidneywart's old fort. It is vacant, and it won't remind you constantly of what you have lost. Maybe with that estate you will attract a lonely giantess." Because he knew from personal experience that women were attracted to men with estates, and there was nothing to abate a man's isolation like a woman.

"Do," the giant agreed.

They parted company, Liverwart going to the stronghold, while Benny and Virtue set out to track down Beranger, who should not be far distant.

"Remind me why I am doing this," he told her.

"You must stop him before he does yet more damage. He has killed my coven and Liverwart's clan; who knows what misery he will bring to others in the future?"

"That's it," Benny agreed. "Oh, I'm forgetting: Cycleze said to cut my hair."

"He did," she agreed. "Yet I wonder why."

"I wonder too. As far as I know, my hair has nothing to do with the rest of my life."

"It doesn't seem to make sense," she agreed. "But he said I could skry it. Maybe I should."

"But you don't have your crystal ball."

"That is merely a convenience. Water will do, here in the field."

"It will?" He tried to picture a ball made of water, but failed.

She led him to the pond where the giants had dipped their water. It was deep, as they needed a lot at a time. She stared down into the quiet depth.

"He was right," she said. "I don't know why, but it is one of the most likely guardians of your life."

Benny believed in her skrying; it wasn't always clear, but it inevitably turned out to be correct. "Then I'd better cut it," he said with real regret. While he had never made an issue of it, he had always been reasonably proud of his silvery locks.

"I will do it. But you won't look nearly so cute. I don't know if I can live with that."

"If you don't stop teasing me, I'll kiss you so hard you'll be sorry."

"Not if I kiss you first." She did so, entirely unmanning him.

She undid his ponytail, letting his hair fall past his shoulders. Then she took her sharp knife that somehow never showed on her body, and carefully cut his locks off close to his scalp. He stood still and suffered, knowing he would look weird.

When the ordeal was done, he peered into the pond. The reflection showed an almost bald-headed boy. What had he expected?

"Ugh," she agreed. "Maybe you'll cause him to laugh to death."

"Will you stop?" he begged.

"Never." She kissed him again, cutely grimacing. "Fortunately I am attracted to more than your hair. Now about the other."

For a moment he was blank. "What other?"

"The berserker bite. That would do it."

Benny reviewed what little he knew of berserkers. Sometimes a man went crazy and started wildly attacking everything within range, seeming insensitive to pain or caution. His reactions were preternaturally swift; no one could stand against him, even if he had not been a strong warrior. No one knew what caused it, or how to stop it. All others could do was stay out of the berserker's way until he either killed himself by falling off a cliff or into a lake, or lost consciousness. If he survived, he was usually okay next day, with no memory of the occasion.

Now a bit of the rationality he had experienced when he smoked the pipe returned to him, and he made sense of the words. "You can cause it with a bite?"

"I did not know it, but once he mentioned it I knew that I could. It would be an extension of the strength bite. I could make you a berserker, for perhaps an hour. Then I think you would be very tired, because it is the resources of your own body that the frenzy draws on."

"And if I held a weapon?"

"You would be unmatchable, and a danger to all around you. I would have to hide until it wore off."

"And if I faced Beranger?"

"You would surely kill him."

Benny pondered that. "No."

"No?"

"It would not be a fair combat. That is not for me."

"But Benny, if you give him a fair chance, that man

99

will kill you. My earlier skrying with the crystal ball is slowly coming clear about that."

"I know it. But if I do not fight fair, I am not worthy of my weapons. Or of you."

"Your conscience leads you to death!"

Benny felt awful. "I know it. I'm sorry."

"And I love you for it. You can't be corrupted by the need to survive or greed for power, which is what this is. That is why Cycleze tried to help you. This is why I can support you, though I abhor violence." Now her eyes overflowed. "But oh, it is hard!"

It occurred to Benny that he could use her emotional healing bite. But he didn't want to ease this crisis of conscience, he wanted to embrace it, difficult as it was to do, and come to the right decision. "It is hard," he agreed.

Now they set out in pursuit of Beranger. The man was injured; there was a sometimes obscure trail of blood. But Benny knew he had resources and would be recovered before long. He had to catch him before that was the case. The berserker ploy seemed unfair, but taking on the man because of his giant killing horror seemed fair. His lingering rationality from the pipe indicated that.

They did not catch up that day. They made camp, ate from their supplies, and slept under a tree. Virtue remained in her human form and clasped him clothed; she wanted to have all she could of him before he got into suicidal combat. He loved that, though he hated the prospect of dying.

In the morning they resumed the pursuit, and it wasn't long before they caught up. "Well, now." It was Beranger, standing across a glade from them. Behind him was a solid building. He must have gone there for some reason. There was no sign of any injury; he must have bound it up once he had time, or found a magic healing potion. "Who the hell are you, bald stranger?"

Benny realized that he had a chance to be anonymous; his shaved head changed his appearance that much. Maybe that was why it was supposed to save his life. But he rejected it. He would live and die as himself. "I am Benny."

"Ah. I know you now." He scowled. "Remember what I told you, kid?"

"That you would kill me if we met again," Benny said.

Beranger glanced past him. "I see you brought your vampire whore along. That should be fun, after you're gone."

He was trying to incite Benny, to make him careless. He was succeeding. "I do have my sword now."

"Good. I'd hate to cut down an unarmed man."

He clearly had no fear of Benny's blade. "You cut down the giants."

"They weren't men."

"True," Benny said grimly. "Some were women. Some were children."

Beranger shrugged. "It isn't as if I haven't taken out women and children before."

And he wasn't even ashamed of it. Cycleze was right; the man had been corrupted. "You're an animal."

"Might as well tell you my side of it, before I dispose of you and despoil your pretty vamp. I knew Cycleze was going to try to kill me, so I killed him first. Fair is fair."

What could Benny say to that? The man was correct on that limited score. "What about the children?"

"I had to get the Alsbury townsmen worked up. That was the fastest way to do it."

"Those children were innocent!"

"Too bad for them. I had a job to do."

"What job could ever justify that?"

"Avenging my brother being killed by those orcs."

"Those orcs were innocent too," Benny said hotly. "They didn't mean to kill your brother. It was an accident."

"That's a lie. If I hadn't stopped the orcs, they would have gone on to kill others."

Which was exactly why Benny had to stop Beranger, ironically. But the man wasn't listening. "So you figure it's okay to murder others you know are innocent, just for the hell of it?"

"Oh, not entirely. There's money to be made from it."

"Money!"

"You saw how we got gold for taking out the zombies and vampires. We got bounties for others, like giants and trolls. Sure, some of them were innocent, at least in the sense that they weren't killing men right then, but Cycleze would cast spells to drive them insane. Then they would attack villages, getting us more work."

As Cycleze had said, he was no saint either. Benny was disgusted anew. "Well, it has to stop."

"Yeah, I guess it's time."

Benny had been afraid for this moment, but now that he was in it, he found that he had no fear, just determination. He did have to kill this man gone rogue. "Protect yourself."

He advanced on Beranger, sword lifted. The man didn't even raise his own blade. "Let's see what you got, kid. You must have practiced in the interim."

Benny showed him. He swung, aiming at the man's neck.

And suddenly his sword was blocked. Beranger had countered him without seeming effort, his motion so swift and sure that Benny had hardly seen it. However corrupt his spirit might be, his body was a finely honed instrument for combat.

Benny tried again and was blocked again. He was hopelessly outclassed, physically.

"My turn," Beranger said. "Consider this a warning. I'm going to make you ugly like me. Your ludicrous bald pate gave me the idea."

Benny never even saw the blade coming at him, but he felt it slice across his face. He heard Virtue scream piercingly. Then he was falling in a haze of blood and pain, knowing he was done for.

Virtue was on him, then, frantically trying to mop up blood, but there was too much of it. She wasn't stanching the flow, she was merely getting it on her face and hands and body. Her lovely long hair was now a mass of gore.

Then she rose into the air, literally. Beranger was hauling her up by her collar. "Now why'd you have to get all messed up like that?" he demanded. "When I just got clean? You make it too messy to mess with you." He dropped her and stomped away.

Benny's consciousness mercifully faded out.

CHAPTER 13

Benny woke up in a monastery-like building. He realized it was the one they had seen before; the fight with Beranger had occurred outside it.

He also realized that his head was on Virtue's lap, cushioned by her warm body. She had her hand on his forehead, and he felt no pain.

"I'm awake," he said. Or tried to; somehow his mouth did not work right, and it came out "Aaahm awaay."

"Do not try to talk," she told him. "We will try to heal you, but that will take time."

"Time?" Aaahm, the same as before.

"I dislike this intensely, but I think you need to know. Look in the mirror." Her hand brought a small round mirror into sight.

Benny looked. He saw his upper face, normal apart from the lack of framing hair. But below his nose was a great gash like that of a walking skeleton, with a few odd teeth projecting. "Whaaah?"

"He cut out your mouth, crosswise," she said. "Your cheeks, teeth, part of your tongue. Your face is like his, only your wound is horizontal."

Benny stared at the gross image, realizing that it was true. He couldn't talk because he had no mouth. Or rather, he had way too much mouth, crossing his face from side to side, incapable of closing properly.

"He made you ugly like him," she said. "It was your baldness that decided him. That is what saved your life. You have no hair to conceal the horror of your face."

He looked at her lovely face beside the mirror. "Oooo?"

"I still love you, Benny," she said. "Never doubt that. But you'll never be cute again. He has seen to that."

Now he remembered. Beranger had said to consider it a warning. Instead of killing him, he had maimed him for life. If they ever met again, then would be the killing.

And what about Virtue herself? "Oooo?" he repeated.

"I was so splattered in your blood that he couldn't touch me that way without getting soiled himself," she said. "So he gave it up as a bad job. That saved me from rape and probably death. I am unharmed, physically."

That was a relief.

"We did what we could to salvage your life before you bled to death," she continued. "We stanched the flow, but you will remain weak until you have had time to renew your blood. We applied healing magic, but could not immediately repair the damage to your mouth. I am sorry, but you will have to be fed liquids with a spoon for some time. The damage is simply too great."

"Weeeee?" Who were the "we" she referred to?

"This is a kind of monastery. The people here are simple hermits and monks who are healers. Beranger came to them to heal the wound in his side; that is why he was here. But your case is worse. They came out immediately to help you and bring you inside, and once you were stable I stripped and washed myself and my dress, and hung it out to dry in the sun." She paused, blushing. "It seemed such a shame to waste your precious spilled blood, so I did lick off your clothing first. It was very tasty, but I hope never to eat your blood again."

"Ooaaaay," he said reassuringly. If anyone was to eat his blood, he wanted it to be her.

"Then I came to hold you, abating your pain so you could sleep and heal. You need much rest and sleep, for now."

An obscure detail lingered in his mind. She had washed her dress, and hung it in the sun to dry. Then come to hold him.

She was holding him now, with no dress on. Nothing on. Just her lustrous hair to help cover her slightly. Her lap was bare, and one breast was cushioning the side of his head. No wonder he felt no pain.

He tried to smile, but the effort only aggravated the wound that was his mouth.

"Now you must sleep some more," she said. She held his head close, and the softness of her breast radiated its own aura of healing.

He slept, mentally smiling despite his injury.

When he woke again, Virtue was clothed, so he knew that some time had passed. He felt stronger, if not actually spry. But something was bothering him.

"Yes, we have been feeding you mead and cider," Virtue said. "Pouring in a few drops at a time. You have taken in a fair amount of liquid, and it does not convert automatically to blood. You will need to pass on the surplus from your digestion. I will help you if you wish, but I think you would prefer to do it by yourself."

Definitely. She helped him climb laboriously to his feet. He got his balance and walked slowly to the door and outside, where he urinated into a convenient bush.

That was enough exercise for the moment. He lay down on the mat and allowed her to hold his head close again, ushering him delightfully into sleep.

The next few days saw him recover nicely, as he got plenty of rest, and Virtue's healing touch restored his body except for his gash of a mouth. The hermit monks brought magic poultices for him to wear outside and inside that mouth, and they rapidly restored lost flesh and some teeth. But it was apparent that he would always have a mouth to make a frog jealous, and his chewing would be limited.

Still, it was better than being dead. Especially since Virtue stood constantly by him, making it clear to all that she was his woman and loved him dearly. He hardly needed to impress any other woman.

He came to know the hermit monks of the monastery. They were humans, orcs, and other sentient beings, male and female, who might have been enemies in the outside world but were friends here. The main ones were miniature humans he thought of as elves, except that they had vestigial wings. Their skin color depended on their roles at the monastery: green for horticulture, herbs and natural healing; red for physician, medical; blue/white for guarding the sick, except that Virtue was doing that for Benny. They wore red caps and simple red loincloths, and called themselves helpers.

Benny realized that the rainbow gnomes on the fresco in the Fox Den were based on these creatures. This gave him a broadened appreciation of the species. They were not mere artist's conceptions; they were real, doing good work.

He practiced diligently, and learned to talk with

reasonable facility, though sometimes he had to hold his hands to his mouth to shape it into certain sounds. It looked awkward, and was slow, but it worked.

An old male helper came to talk with him, as he sat beside Virtue. The helper was purple, subtly denoting divine royalty. His wings were as white as snow, and instead of wearing a red cap and loincloth he wore a gold cloth. This was the one Benny took to be the eldest monk, who called himself Search. "I am searching for enlightenment, if not salvation," he said candidly. "I believe I am finding it here, dedicating my life to humble service to others. We do what we can for anyone who asks for help."

"That's why you healed Beranger," Benny said carefully, making sure the words came out correctly.

"Yes. He was injured, and we were able to make him almost well again, physically."

"But he has slaughtered many innocent creatures and people, even children."

"We do not ask a person's history. That is not our business. We care only that a person needs our help, and we give that freely, asking in return that they do us no harm while here. We do not see ourselves as superior to the other sapient races, only different; we are servants, not masters."

"That's why you took in the two of us," Benny said. "A severely injured man and a vampire."

"A good man, as we understand it. And a good vampire." He quirked a smile. "A very pretty one."

Virtue smiled back. "Thank you."

Benny had seen the monks glancing at Virtue, not with desire but with appreciation, for she seemed to brighten the region where she stood. She was probably the prettiest woman ever to grace the monastery. He understood perfectly. "Her character is even lovelier than her body."

"So we gather," Search said. "You will do as you choose, of course, but we would be quite satisfied to have both of you remain here, and become helpers, if you choose. There is goodness in you."

"I think we will be going home, once we complete our mission," Benny said. "But we do appreciate the offer, and know that residence here would be far from the worst we could do. Whether you would want us, if you knew our histories, is another matter."

"We make it a point not to pry, but we are curious, if you care to tell us."

So Benny told him how he had traveled with the two rough men, then interceded to save Virtue's life, and finally tried unsuccessfully to stop Beranger from doing more harm. Virtue filled in her story of her life with the coven. "You would have liked the other vampires," she said. "They tried to do good, much as you are trying. But fate was not kind to them."

"Perhaps they would have succeeded better if they had joined the Protector, as we have," Search said.

"I would like to know more of this being," Virtue said, and Benny was curious too.

"You have asked, and I am glad to tell. The Protector is our God, who governs and benefits all, especially those who devote themselves to him."

"All?" Benny asked skeptically. "Even children?"

"Especially children."

"I'm sorry, but I just can't believe in a deity that would allow the children at Alsbury, or the innocent orcs, vampires, and giants, to be brutally killed," Benny said hotly. "If he is real, he should protect them from such abuse."

"Ah, but it is not so simple," Search said. "I too wondered at that, as I have seen many injustices in this world, but I have learned that managing the larger frame is no easy chore, even for one with phenomenal powers of observation and action. Sometimes compromise is necessary, unfortunate as it may seem to others. The Protector does watch over all, but he also desires the several species to watch over each other and do right by each other. He gives them as much freedom to fulfill themselves as possible, but that also increases the chances of their drifting from the preferred path. When they go astray he mourns, but the alternative would be to hold them to too tight a leash and not allow them to be all that they can be. Freedom and responsibility go hand in hand. It is sad that no living thing is truly innocent, but at least real good will never truly die. When this necessary compromise leads to mischief, as it so often does, and the bodies of children and others are destroyed, they do live on with the Protector. So the children you mourn are not truly dead, they merely have been relegated to another realm, the spiritual one."

"This sounds like casuistry to me," Benny said. "To pretend that those who die are not truly dead. How convenient!"

"You doubt," Search said, unperturbed. "As I did. Doubt is good; it signals an active mind. But the Protector is not like other deities, who have been anthropomorphized and corrupted; he is above matter itself. We in this single plane see only those who pass through it, and not the larger nature of their being. If we could see the whole of creation, we would be vastly reassured."

"I see your point," Virtue said. "It makes me feel better about the loss of my coven."

"Well, I don't see it," Benny said. "There ought to be a way to spare the innocent from abuse and slaughter. Any god who wants my respect should see to that."

"This is something every man or other intelligent being must figure out for himself," Search said. "Just as every person must find the unique magic that is within him or her."

"Magic?" Benny said. "Virtue has magic, but I have none."

"Ah, but you are mistaken, Benny," Search said. "Every person has magic, and you are no exception. Virtue knows."

"Benny has magic," Virtue agreed. "I feel it in him. But I have no idea what it is."

"Because he has not yet discovered and invoked it." He smiled at Benny. "I leave you to that process." He departed.

Benny found himself unsatisfied with his own position. Next day he looked for Search, but did not see him. "Please, where is Search?" he asked another monk.

"Who?"

"Search. The purple monk we talked with yesterday, in the gold loincloth."

"There is no monk by that name or description here."

Benny stared at him. "But we talked with him. He gave us the philosophy of the monastery. He told us about the Protector."

But all the monks agreed: there was no such person here. The Protector was real, but he had no physical manifestation.

Virtue put her hand on his, reassuringly. She knew that Search was real and tangible, just as Benny did. But for some reason he wasn't known here in that form.

Later they discussed it privately. "I did feel the magic in Search's being," Virtue said. "I thought it was his aura of holiness, his dedication to the work of the monastery. Now I wonder if it wasn't something more."

"More?"

"They say that the Protector has no physical presence. Maybe they just don't see it. Maybe he shows himself only to those who need to see. The imperfect ones who are searching for him, maybe without knowing it."

"This is fantasy!" Benny said. But there was a thread of continuing wonder in him. Certainly Search was real. Why had he come to Benny and Virtue?

In due course Benny healed in everything except his gaping mouth. It was time to move on. They made ready.

Search appeared. "Wait two more days," he said. He touched Virtue's hand. Then he was gone, though they did not see him go. Naturally no one else had seen him.

"I think he is an agent of God," Virtue said, staring at her hand. "I felt divinity."

An agent of God. Benny was almost able to accept that.

They waited two days, helping the helpers with stray chores. A woman great with child came, unable to birth her baby. Virtue put her hand on her forehead, and the woman relaxed, and then the baby came. A nearby man was in pain; Benny went into the forest and found him with a badly smashed foot, and supported him so that he could make it into the monastery where the helpers could help him.

Then came grim news: there had been another atrocity. The house of a sisterhood of sylphs had been raided by a severely scarred man, the sylphs raped, and their home burned down.

"Beranger is signaling us," Benny said angrily. "He is daring me to come and try to stop him."

"He must be stopped," Virtue agreed.

"That's why Search told us to wait," Benny said. "So I would get the news and be ready to go, instead of being out of touch somewhere else."

They set out immediately, traveling toward the sylph community. Sylphs were lovely delicate female entities, dedicated to caring for minor forest creatures. There was no reason ever to hurt one.

Benny struggled with his conscience. "I felt it would be unfair to take advantage of your berserker bite," he told Virtue. "But if that's what it takes to stop this menace, then I must do it. There is no sense getting myself killed and you raped, which is what will happen otherwise."

"Yes," she agreed simply.

"I think this time I'll use a club. They are better for mindless violence." He scouted around and found a stout fallen branch that would do.

They arrived the following morning. The sylphs were gone, having fled the horror stalking them, but Beranger remained. Beranger's hair had grown significantly since Benny last saw him, shooting out like tentacles, and the man's eyes jerked constantly in every direction. 'Bout time you showed up, you and your vamp whore," the man said. He hefted his massive magic spiked club, "This time I'll make sure there's no blood for her to muck in. I knew I'd get her if I brought you in." There was no doubt that he had a thing for Virtue, an ugly thing.

"Bite me," Benny murmured.

Virtue put her fang to his shoulder and bit. He felt the rush of it immediately, spreading through his body.

There were no other preliminaries. Benny advanced on Beranger, holding his makeshift club.

Beranger paused, assessing him. "Uh-oh. I didn't figure

Piers Anthony/Kenneth Kelly

on a berserker. I didn't know she could do that."

Benny was now well into it. He didn't talk, he just waded in. He swung viciously at Beranger's head. The man barely got his club up in time to block it.

"They say that no man can stand against a berserker," Beranger continued. He smiled as he fended off another blow. "Except another berserker."

Then he changed. Saliva dripped from the base of his mouth, and his eyes turned lambent. He was turning berserker himself!

Now Benny understood why the man was such a devastating warrior. He could turn berserker at will, and demolish his opponents with unparalleled viciousness.

So it was berserker versus berserker. The two were evenly matched. Except for one thing: Benny's club was impromptu, while Beranger's club was a finely crafted and battle tested instrument. Each time the two clubs met, a bit of Benny's club flaked off. Soon he would be without a feasible weapon.

He had to finish this fast, before that happened. He increased his fury, battering madly at the other man. Beranger was hard put to defend himself, but Benny could not quite put him away.

He struck one more blow—and club met club, and his own club shattered, leaving only a stump in his hand. It had happened. He had lost his weapon, and thus the match.

Beranger swung at him, and Benny had no defense. Yet somehow it was not in him to retreat. He stood there, waiting for the end.

Virtue screamed.

The club came at his head, and Benny was frozen in place. Then something odd happened. It was as if time stood still.

He saw Search, standing behind Beranger. And somehow he knew that Search was not merely God's representative, but God himself. *What is your will?* he asked mentally, knowing that he was about to find out whether there was an afterlife and what his place in it might be.

Find your magic. And Search was gone.

Virtue's scream continued as the passage of time resumed. Benny focused as the club came at his head. Then he felt his magic.

The club passed his head without contact. Beranger stumbled, off-balanced by the lack of resistance. Somehow he had missed.

Benny whacked Beranger's head with the stump of his club, and the man went down. It had not been a brain-splattering blow, but it had been hard enough.

Virtue's scream ended.

Benny stood, looking down at the unconscious man. He had won! But why had Beranger's blow missed? That should not have happened.

Virtue ran to join him. "He didn't miss," she said, knowing Benny's thought.

"But then--"

"The club passed right through you. You became a ghost! That's your magic."

"I'm not a ghost," Benny protested. "I'm as solid as ever."

"For only an instant. Just long enough."

He realized that it was true. He had invoked his ability to discorporate, and it had saved his life. Because Search had been there to give him the clue.

"I found my magic," he agreed as the berserker rage

faded. "Because--"

"I saw Search. I heard him tell you. Now I know he is God."

"He is God," Benny agreed, his belief now complete.

Chapter 14

"Now what do we do with Dale?" Virtue asked. Beranger lay unconscious, his deadly club reverted to its small metal rod form.

"I guess I'm supposed to kill him," Benny said uneasily. "Maybe in the heat of battle I could, but now that he's down, I don't know."

"I have an idea. He could be a good man, if only his bad side didn't rule him. I think he might have spared me before not just because of the blood, but because there was a spark of decency that made him look for a pretext to let me go. If he were good instead of sadly mixed, he could go back to the inn and marry Nadia. That would become the reason Jack thought she would benefit by associating with me. I could bite him, to kill that bad side only."

"You can do that?" he asked, amazed.

"I think I can. It was one of the things we studied in the coven. But he would have to agree. We're not supposed to do such things unasked. I'm not sure he would accept."

Beranger stirred. They didn't have much time.

"This much I think I can do," Benny said. He picked up his sword. "Dale Beranger," he said.

The man looked up dizzily. "Huh?"

"I defeated you in combat. I now give you a choice: accept Virtue's bite to eliminate your bad side, or die. One or the other. If you try to move, I will cut off your head." He held his sword ready. It was not a bluff; he knew better than to let the man go without severe reform. Their lives would be the forfeit.

Beranger considered. "I don't want to be a vampire."

"This is not a vampire bite," Virtue said. "It is a death-to-evil bite. The bad in you will be expunged, and only the good will remain."

"No other change?" Beranger asked.

"No other change," Virtue assured him. "But you will become an entirely different man."

"Sure, then, why not."

Benny was wary. Beranger was agreeing too readily. He meant to grab Virtue when she came close to do the bite, maybe using her as a shield against Benny's sword. "Then lie down prone, hands by your sides," Benny said. "If you move from that position before she bites you, I will cut off your head. Do you care to gamble that I am bluffing?"

Beranger squinted at him, assessing the odds. He knew that moving would signal his return to combat, putting Benny in combat mode. He realized that it was a bad bet. He stretched out on the ground, hands at his sides. But he might move those hands swiftly when she got close. For a brief moment, Benny saw that the scar on Beranger's forehead had begun to bleed, split apart from the boy's winning blow.

"Bite his leg," Benny said tersely.

Virtue nodded. The man could not grab her with his legs. Not from that position.

Benny stood with sword ready to chop down on the

neck. Virtue got down and put her face to one calf. She paused. Beranger did not move. Maybe he was waiting until she actually touched him to make his play. When she was committed to the bite.

Virtue's head dropped down so suddenly it was a blur. Her fangs stabbed the calf and withdrew.

Beranger rolled over almost as swiftly, grabbing for her as he jerked his head away from Benny's sword. But she was already out of reach, having anticipated this treachery. Benny stepped forward, ready to swing.

"Wait," Virtue warned. Benny stopped.

Beranger scrambled to his feet, stood a moment, then fell down again. He writhed on the ground.

"What's he doing?" Benny asked nervously.

"His good and evil sides are warring against each other," Virtue answered. "But it is too late. My bite gives the good side power to defeat the bad side. It will be over soon."

She was right. Beranger stopped writhing and relaxed. "My name is Dale. Will you believe me if I tell you you can trust me now?" he asked.

"Yes, Dale," Virtue said, walking up to him.

"Wait!" Benny said, not at all trusting this.

But the man did not try to grab her or strike her. "Would you believe me if I thanked you for freeing me from the monster?"

"Yes."

"I am indeed a changed man."

"I know," Virtue said. "Now we will take you back to Gant, to the inn, where Nadia waits for you."

"The sexy barmaid? What does she want with me?"

"She wants to marry you. This is one of the compensations for going to the light side."

119

Dale considered. "I think not."

Benny gripped his sword, alarmed, but Virtue was unconcerned. "Why not? She is a most attractive young woman."

"That she is. But I am not an attractive man."

"She doesn't care about your scar, any more than I care about Benny's scar."

"It's the evil I have done. I can't rest until that is expunged."

For a moment Virtue froze, and Benny knew she was remembering her slaughtered coven. Then she recovered. "That can't be done."

"I know it, but maybe I can make up for it by saving as many lives as I destroyed, so that there is a balance of my account. That will take me a lifetime, if I can do it at all. I will be busy. Too busy to settle down with a good woman, however much I might like to. She will have to find another man."

"She will do nothing of the kind," Virtue said evenly. "She will marry your burden of debt when she marries you, and help you abate it."

"But she'll never be able to rest!"

"I know her, Dale. She is looking for her mission in life. This will be it. She will be restless with you, for life, until it is settled."

He was taken aback. "I do not deserve this."

Virtue smiled. "You will earn it. You assume that you must be miserable until your accounts balance. This is not the case. You can be happy. The point is that you will constantly be doing good. That will gratify you."

Slowly he nodded. "You seem to know something about doing good."

"It is my orientation. Now let's be on our way."

Dale glanced at Benny. Benny shrugged, similarly bemused. Could it really be this clear-cut? Or was Virtue inverting things in her desire to help people? He couldn't be sure, but he loved her for it. Her inner beauty outshone her external beauty, impossible as that might seem.

They got on their way. Dale did indeed seem to be a changed man, behaving perfectly, not even looking at Virtue except when he spoke with her. When they made camp for the night, he did more than his share, hacking poles to make a lean-to and collecting wood for a cookfire. Could he be faking it?

"Your distrust does not become you," Virtue murmured.

"I'm sorry."

She smiled, then went to the nearby stream where she stripped and washed. The very water seemed to flow more brightly from her touch. Dale ignored her. If it was an act, it was complete.

In the night there was a nearby howling. Dale was immediately on his feet, sword in hand, sniffing the air. "Werewolves on the hunt," he said. "Not coming this way." He lay down again.

It would be a foolish werewolf who attacked such a man. It seemed that the light side was just as competent with a weapon as the dark side.

They arrived at the Fox Den by mid-morning. The halfling Nap came out to greet them. "Who are you, frogface?" he demanded of Benny.

Virtue stepped forward and kissed him on the top of the head. "That's Benny. I cut his hair, and he got injured in a fight."

"Oh." Nap looked away, embarrassed by his own

reaction. Then he dashed inside to tell Jack.

In moments both Jack and Nadia emerged. The two girls hugged. Then Virtue introduced the men. "This is Benny after a bad fight. This is Dale, who has turned from the dark side to the light side. He will marry Nadia."

"Oh!" Nadia exclaimed, taken aback.

"I have to tell you--" Dale began.

"That he has a mission to do as much good as he has already done harm," Virtue said. "He will be quite busy."

"I'll help!" Nadia said promptly.

Dale had trouble believing that. "But there's so much, and I'll have to travel so far, you probably won't want to--"

"Kiss him," Virtue said. "That will shut him up."

Nadia strode forward and kissed Beranger. He shut up. Benny knew how that sort of thing was. Women had special magic.

In due course they told Jack, Nadia, and Nap the whole story. Then the giant Liverwart arrived, visiting from his new stronghold. He paused when he saw Beranger.

"Dale has changed," Virtue said. "He is sorry for what he did to my coven and your clan, and means to make amends. He will help you find a pretty giantess to share your residence."

"Uh, yes, sure," Dale agreed, surprised. "I know where there are some giant lasses just coming of age. I'll take you there."

Liverwart looked at Benny. "Do?"

What could he say? "Do."

The giant trusted Benny and Virtue. He took off his shirt, which was a huge purple tunic with white polka dots, converted from a bed sheet, and put it on Dale as a sign of acceptance. In the mountain giant culture that was a sign of love, respect, and forgiveness. At any other time, Benny would've laughed at how ridiculous Dale looked, but for Dale and Liverwart this was a very serious matter.

"I will try to earn this," Dale said, moved.

In the afternoon Liverwart, Nadia, and Dale set off for the locale of the giantesses. Benny and Virtue took over Nadia's duties at the inn, serving and entertaining the customers. They even did a little dance, a sort of beauty and the beast, which was warmly received. Folk were getting used to Benny's new appearance.

And one of those customers was Search, the purple gnome with wings. Benny froze in amazement. "I—what are you doing here?" he asked inanely.

"Do not be concerned," Search replied. "The others here are not perceiving this dialogue at all. We are private." Because no one saw Search unless he chose to be seen.

Benny, knocked off his mental equilibrium, tried to be funny. "I thought the protector had no real form." But it came out querulous rather than humorous.

"This is true," Search said. "I can take on many forms. I am using the one that is familiar to you. I use other forms to be familiar to other folk. My truest and original form is far beyond anything the sentient races can imagine."

"It is?" Benny continued to flounder, not knowing what to make of this. Why should this divine person brace him here in the tavern? His mind was clear; he wasn't even drinking the ale, just serving it.

For answer, Search shifted into a dazzling spiral of light that bathed the whole room with fluorescing patterns of color. This became a star going gloriously nova, then a slowly turning galaxy of scintillating constellations. Benny had no knowledge of such things, yet he recognized them as he saw them. He stood transfixed by the sheer wonder of the scene.

The images coalesced back into the gnome. "Now you understand," Search said.

"Now I believe," Benny said. He had once been skeptical, and was no more. "But why are you coming to me?"

"You and yours have business to accomplish," Search said. "I thought I should let you know."

Benny could not imagine what business. "Uh—will I ever see you again?" Suddenly that was extremely important. "I mean, in this life?"

"Yes, though perhaps not in a familiar form. I will come to you at need, as defined by me, to see that you are able to accomplish my designs."

"Uh--" But he stopped, because Search had faded out. He was back with the customers, who were impatient for their ale.

Benny remained confused, but also reassured. His hitherto somewhat aimless life was assuming some meaning. That, plus Virtue, was all he needed.

EPILOGUE

The Pawben awoke from his reflections almost immediately upon feeling something rest on his right shoulder. In his years since coming to Golden Mulch Wood, he'd never known bandits to prowl in the area, but it wouldn't be the first time someone had come upon him unawares. With a speed that deceived his years, he dropped his pipe and grabbed at what he thought was a man's hand, thinking to pull him around and throttle him to the floor. Instead, he heard a squeal and saw a mass of grey fur go flying into the corner of the room. The huge rat then scurried off, back out the front door. Pawben heard the cackling of the little boy he had seen playing with the rat earlier, and turned upon him.

"Gotcha!" The boy yelled. He turned on his heels and ran back out the door to find his companion.

"He's a Beranger, alright." Pawben laughed. The boy certainly had the mischief of his grandfather Dale.

Back at the window, he resumed munching on the roll he'd started earlier. Remembering made him hungry. Feeling a twinge of pain, he rubbed his cheeks where the remnants of the nearly forgotten scar had been. Time and magic had healed it significantly since Dale Beranger had given it to him in centuries prior, but occasionally a spark of pain would shoot across his face, and he was never quite able to forget the horrors of his past.

"If Virtue could see this old codger, now."

He thought again of the countless friends and companions: Dale, Liverwart, Nadia, Laughing Jack, Virtue, and even annoying little Nap. They were all gone now, some passing peacefully in old age, while others had perished in battle and sickness. It was too much to think of all at once, but he found it necessary to occasionally ponder the events of his past, his memory of which was helped by the magical pipe Cycleze had once used. He had to remember. He had to remember because Dale's son, on his deathbed, had made Pawben promise to watch over the little boy, his son, and to keep him safe. Pawben had adventured in many worlds since the events in this most recent flashback, and thought this present one to be the most peaceful in which to raise the boy. Maybe one day he would take the kid back to the land of his forefathers, but the later memories of what befell there were far too painful to take the boy back now. For an instant he remembered Search, and the things he had said. Pawben hadn't seen Search since that day in the Fox Den, or at least if he had, Search had chosen to remain anonymous. Either way, Pawben remembered the things he had taught him, and he had never lost faith in the Protector.

"Is it that time, already?" Pawben said as he noticed the faintest glimmer of a setting sun through the forest.

He had promised to join Toadstoole Tortoisse that afternoon for dinner and a fine game of checkers, and Pawben hated being late. He finished the roll, not wanting to be wasteful, and grabbed his traveling pouch. It would take a few hours to get to Toadstool's, and he'd probably stay the night.

"Come, boy! We're going to Toadstool's for dinner!" he yelled. The little boy came scurrying around the corner, the huge rat hot on his heels.

"Can Flack come too?" the boy asked, indicating the rat.

"I suppose, but don't let Toadstool catch you feeding him from the table again. He doesn't like that."

The three walked out onto the main path, the Pawben walking with his arm around the boy, and the rat on the little kid's shoulder. Almost like a giant, and a man, and a bat, so long ago.

"Tell me about Flack again, Pawben." The boy said.

"Flack? You found that little rascal digging in my turnips, or have you forgotten?" Pawben's memory had failed him briefly.

"No, I mean the other Flack, the one you named the rat after."

Pawben's memory sparked back to life, and sorrow filled his heart when he realized whom the boy was speaking of.

"Another time, lad," he said, "another time."

Author's Note: Piers Anthony

I have done more than 30 book collaborations over the years. Why do I get into them? As a challenge, and for the sake of a given story, and sometimes just to help another writer. *Virtue Inverted* is an example of the last. Kenneth Kelly, a Florida author of the science fiction novel *Trespassing Through Time*, had a fantasy project that had blocked up. These things happen; I once wrote two novels in a trilogy, *Omnivore* and *Orn*, then got hung up on the third and waited six years until inspiration came for *OX*. So I said to Ken send it to me, and I would unblock it. What arrogance made me say that about a book I had never seen? Well, I have an asset I was pretty sure Ken lacked: more than half a century of commercial writing experience. I'm a slow learner, but in that amount of time I have pretty well learned how to fix a problem project. So he sent it, and I did.

Who did what? He started it, and summarized the rest, and I filled in what was needed to make it complete. I felt it was weak on romance, so I enhanced that aspect. Virtue Vampire not only became a more important character, she contributed to the title. I tried to make her the kind of vampire any normal man would want for a girlfriend or wife, startling as that might seem before you get to know her. It will be for the readers to decide whether I succeeded.

As for me personally, I am at this writing 80 years old but not at all ready to go gentle into that good night. I am agnostic, and have no expectation of any life beyond this one, in contrast to my collaborator, so I'm trying to make this life count. I live on my small tree farm with my wife of 59 years and seldom go more than 30 miles from home. I am known primarily for my Xanth fantasy series, despite having no personal belief in magic, and my interests are hardly limited to that. Again, as I write this, the New Horizons space mission is sending back pictures of the planet Pluto and its large moon Charon, and I am quite glad to be alive to see them. Back in my day, Pluto was Mickey's Mouse's dog, but I was always a fan of the planet too, and wrote a story about it in sixth grade. So my life still has things to pick up on.

Readers who want to know more of me can find me at my web site, www.HiPiers.com, where I run a monthly blog-type column calculated to aggravate anyone with any reasonable wit, and an ongoing survey of electronic publishers and related services, with no holds barred feedback on good and bad publishers, intended to assist writers who have dreams without publishers. I remember how it was; from the time I made my decision to be a professional writer, it took me a college BA in creative writing and eight years to make my first sale. When I fought to get an honest accounting from my first novel publisher

I got blacklisted for six years. I'm not sure it's easier now, and time has not mellowed me much.

Virtue Inverted was proofread by Scott M Ryan and Anne White.

Now get on to the next Author Note to meet Ken Kelly.

Author's Note:
Kenneth Kelly

I was in 10th grade when I read my first Xanth novel: *Demons Don't Dream*. Ever since then, I have been a huge fan of Piers Anthony and fantasy in general. I've been writing and telling stories all my life. Even before I could write, I would tell my parents tales, and they would write them down for me. It is a true passion, but I know that my skills in the craft aren't perfect. Thus, I asked Mr. Anthony to help.

I earned a BA in English Professional Writing from Saint Leo University in St. Leo, Fl in 2013, and shortly after published my first completed novel, *Trespassing Through Time*. After reading my book, Mr. Anthony allowed me to send him an unfinished manuscript that would become *Virtue Inverted*. I had begun the book in 12th grade of high school, and although my skills in writing still need work, I quickly realized that this old draft needed a major overhaul. After collecting dozens of handwritten chapters and notes – some of which I had forgotten about – I played around with the characters and story, and outlined the rest for Mr. Anthony. I am not ashamed to admit that for me to have tried and typed the rest would have been complete disaster. Piers Anthony gave me a chance when I doubt many other novelists would. God bless him for that.

Mr. Anthony is Agnostic, and I consider myself a Christian, as some have probably surmised from the contents of this book. My intentions for adding these themes were not done in hopes of converting Mr. Anthony or any readers, although I would be happy if the themes in this book helped some in this aspect. I included these ideas because my beliefs are a large part of who I am, and because I want the readers to know me personally. For many, this book will be nothing more than good fiction. In reality, that's all it is. But, I hope at least a few people will find something more in these words, as I found in Mr. Anthony's writings.

Despite the shabbiness of its original draft, I put a ton of work into this book, which Mr. Anthony helped build into the finished product. I thank him, the readers, and countless others for inspiring and motivating me to continue my writing, especially Mr. Schism from Plant City High School, who in my 12th grade English class read the book's initial chicken scratch. I hope Mr. Anthony and I remain friends for many years to come, and that he will be gracious enough to let me work with him on future projects.

ABOUT THE AUTHORS

Piers Anthony is one of the world's most popular fantasy authors, and a New York Times bestseller twenty-one times over. Anthony is the author of the Xanth series, as well as many other best-selling works. Piers Anthony lives with his wife in Inverness, Florida.

Kenneth Kelly is a 26 year old native of Plant City, Fl. He has been an avid writer his whole life, and has had a number of short works published during grade school and college. He has a Bachelors degree in English Professional Writing from St. Leo University. He is the author of 'Trespassing Through Time.' Outside of writing he is a 3rd degree black belt in Tar Kwon Do.